s

SO MANY **BOYS**

SO MANY **BOYS**

suzanne young

razOr
bill

An Imprint of Penguin Group (USA) Inc.

So Many Boys

RAZORBILL

Published by the Penguin Group
Penguin Young Readers Group
345 Hudson Street, New York, New York 10014, U.S.A.
Penguin Group (USA) Inc., 375 Hudson Street, New York, New York 10014, U.S.A.
Penguin Group (Canada), 90 Eglinton Avenue East, Suite 700, Toronto, Ontario,
Canada M4P 2Y3 (a division of Pearson Penguin Canada Inc.)
Penguin Books Ltd, 80 Strand, London WC2R 0RL, England
Penguin Ireland, 25 St Stephen's Green, Dublin 2, Ireland
(a division of Penguin Books Ltd)
Penguin Group (Australia), 250 Camberwell Road, Camberwell, Victoria 3124,
Australia (a division of Pearson Australia Group Pty Ltd)
Penguin Books India Pvt Ltd, 11 Community Centre,
Panchsheel Park, New Delhi – 110 017, India
Penguin Group (NZ), 67 Apollo Drive, Rosedale, North Shore 0632, New Zealand
(a division of Pearson New Zealand Ltd.)
Penguin Books (South Africa) (Pty) Ltd, 24 Sturdee Avenue,
Rosebank, Johannesburg 2196, South Africa

Penguin Books Ltd, Registered Offices: 80 Strand, London WC2R 0RL, England

10 9 8 7 6 5 4 3 2 1

Library of Congress Cataloging-in-Publication Data is available.

Printed in the United States of America

For my grandmother Josephine Parzych.

This is for you.

Always.

SOS
UNDER NEW MANAGEMENT

Dear Clients,

I'm happy to announce the re-forming of SOS. Due to a change in leadership, services were temporarily put on hold. But now we're back and totally badass.

If your boyfriend is acting suspicious, text a cheater-request form to our new number at 555-1863, but be specific. For us to catch him in the act, we'll need to know exactly who he's doing.

Again, we're psyched to help out the girls of Washington in their quest for a decent boyfriend. We're currently updating our Naughty List roster, so text with any important information.

There is now a fee schedule for our services, but for the grand reopening, we'll offer a fifty percent discount to the first ten clients.

We're back. And we're going to kick cheating ass.

SOS–XOXO
SOS
Text: 555-1863
Exposing Cheaters for Over Three Years

ASSIGNMENT 1

1:00 A.M., SEPTEMBER 12

A branch splintered under the operative's heavy boot, cracking loud enough to make her pause. After a quick look around Riley Richards's back lawn, she continued her path toward his half-open bedroom window.

Even from the yard, she could hear their soft murmurs. She crouched down in the wet soil of the flower bed, taking out the night-vision goggles she'd stolen. Silently she clicked on the viewfinder and peered in.

The suspect, Riley, was in there along with his accomplice, Megan Wright. They were sitting on his bed (fully clothed), talking. *Talking?*

The operative narrowed her eyes and shifted in the dirt. This was not what she'd anticipated. Proof might take longer than previously thought, and the black latex jumpsuit she'd snatched was getting filthy.

When she'd found the SOS files and gone through them, the operative had seen a problem—a reason why SOS wasn't as effective as it could've been. The society was set up to be secret, completely undercover. And that was the problem. It left no room for intimidation. And if the operative hoped to make SOS her own success—and outshine Tessa Crimson—she'd have to fix that. She had a plan.

Clicking off a few stills, the operative listened patiently. Megan was looking sideways at Riley as they sat hip-to-hip on his navy blue comforter.

"So, do you want to work on that chemistry lab?" Megan asked, twisting a long strand of blonde hair around her finger.

The left side of Riley's mouth twitched. "Not really."

"But I thought you said—"

"I wanted to see you," he interrupted. "But I knew you wouldn't if I didn't say it was for school."

Megan bit her lip. "Jenn's my friend," she whispered. "You know that." She shifted uncomfortably, moving away from the suspect. "I shouldn't even be here right now."

But when Megan didn't get up to leave, the operative tensed, finger poised over the viewfinder. No matter how Riley got her to his house, Megan obviously wanted to be there. This was about to become a full-fledged cheat.

"I'm sorry," Riley whispered, reaching out to touch Megan's arm. "I know this is hard, but...I like you, Meg. Don't you like me?"

The operative paused on the record button as she suddenly became fascinated with the developing relationship. Sure, Riley was propositioning Meg, but not really—not in a way that offered real proof. Liking someone wasn't the same as adultery. Not unless Megan agreed to go through with it. Would she?

"I..." Megan stopped long enough to make it clear she didn't want to say what she was about to. "I should go."

"Please," Riley murmured, taking her hand. "Don't leave yet."

Outside, the operative watched, knots forming in her stomach as she waited to see if they'd cheat. In the SOS files she'd found the official tally sheets. Tessa Crimson had caught more than two hundred cheaters. The operative tightened her jaw. It would be hard to beat Tessa at her own game when she played it so damn well.

Just then Megan's ring tone filled the darkened room with the latest drama-club anthem, something by *Journey*. Megan reached into her pocket to look at her caller ID, then drew in a quick breath.

"It's Jenn," she said.

Riley let his hand drop from Megan's as she clicked off her phone and slid it self-consciously back into her jeans.

Riley sighed. "I'll walk you out."

The operative was disappointed. She chewed hard on the corner of her thumbnail, lost in thought. If she was going to take over SOS and make it what it should be, she'd need to out-spy the former team. But this mission hadn't offered the sort of evidence she'd need to confirm Jenn's suspicions, and more troubling than that was the fact that Megan had resisted. Cheaters weren't supposed to resist. Until now, there'd been a one-hundred percent infidelity rate. The operative was counting on that to continue.

As soon as Riley's bedroom door had closed behind the suspects, the operative stood up in the flower bed and slid her body through the open window.

Ouch! She looked down to see that the fabric around her thigh had snagged on the sill and ripped a hole in her suit, leaving a long scratch. Irritated, she straightened, glancing around the room for Riley's computer. When she spotted it, she walked over and inserted the CD she'd hidden in her cleavage.

When it was in, the operative clicked Run. It would copy Riley's entire hard drive—every program, every picture, every application. There must be something of value in there, something incriminating.

The operative tapped her boot as she waited. The computer beeped, and she bent down to look at the screen. *Wipe complete.* She hit the space bar a few times, but nothing else came up.

"Shit," she murmured, reaching over to eject the CD. She examined the disc carefully. Oh, no! She'd accidentally inserted the data eraser. She shook her head, reaching up to bite her nail again as she considered her problem.

She looked around the room for any other collectible data, hoping the mission wouldn't be a total loss. Then she saw it. Riley's phone was resting on his dresser.

Walking over, she removed the battery and took out the SIM card, slipping it into her bra once she had it. With a satisfied sigh, she pulled a tiny listening device from her pocket, looking it over as she traipsed toward the open window. She brought it up to her lips and kissed it, leaving a tiny smudge of red across the surface. Then she peeled back the adhesive and stuck it under the edge of Riley's desk as she passed.

Riley and Megan might not have been cheating, but there was clearly intent. The operative needed this confirmation. She would just have to keep watching them, because sooner or later, they'd slip up.

Cheaters always did.

CHAPTER ONE

I PLACED MY PALMS ON THE CUSHY PINK YOGA MAT on the floor of my living room. Stretching my legs out behind me, I pushed my body up into the triangular pose of downward dog. The dark waves of my hair hung down, tickling my face as I extended farther, feeling the pull that always loosened my tense muscles. Sigh.

"Oh, I like that position," Aiden called from the couch.

I tumbled back to the floor. It was hard to hold the pose with Aiden in the room. "Be nice," I said, glancing over at him. He looked adorable. His blond floppy curls had been cropped short, and his green eyes sparkled in the Sunday morning light. And to be honest, I loved that he loved the view.

"Nice? You hate when I'm nice," he said, tilting his head. "Now come over here and let me be naughty."

I laughed and sat back on my heels. When my parents decided to spend the weekend in Seattle to celebrate their anniversary, Aiden had graciously volunteered to keep me company. We were…*working on our relationship.*

"You all flexible now?" he asked with a smile, holding his hand out to me. "Because I'd like a kiss."

Aiden and I had enjoyed a very relaxing weekend together, but I'd made it a point to set boundaries. For example, as long as

we were together but not officially dating, there would be no…
home runs. He'd said that was fine. Even though I missed the Pink
Champagne toenail polish exchanges we used to have, it was less
complicated this way.

"One kiss," I said. "But then I have to call—" When I slid my
palm into Aiden's, there was a small pinch in my lower back—
a muscle spasm. It made my breath catch, and Aiden pulled me
to him, looking concerned.

"Everything okay?"

I nodded, rubbing my back as Aiden leaned forward to kiss my
neck. "See," he murmured. "You're still taking on too much."

I closed my eyes as his hot breath touched my skin. "No, I'm
not." I had no idea what this recent muscle spasm was about,
but I doubted it had anything to do with helping people in the
name of self-recovery. "Besides," I said. "I can't just abandon
everything."

"You should," Aiden said, pulling back before wrapping his
arms around me.

"Including you?" I asked, raising my eyebrow.

He grinned. "Not me, baby. I'm a keeper. Remember?"

I laughed. "That's right. I forgot." But my laugh was hollow. I
couldn't exactly *keep* what I didn't *have*.

"Now come here," Aiden growled as he tackled me back onto
the couch. Temporarily forgetting my doubts, I wrapped my legs
around his waist (thank you, yoga) as he tried to tickle me.

"Seriously," I said after a few minutes, even though I was pretty
sure that I was the one holding him to me. "I only have a sec."

"Then we'd better hurry," he whispered. I closed my eyes.

It had been three months, one week, and two days since I'd
been a Smitten Kitten. I'd quit the squad (although I kept the

uniform for personal reasons) at the beginning of the summer, leaving it in Kira's perfectly polished hands.

Since the incident at Aiden's house last year—including the unfortunate stitch to my forehead—my parents suffered from terrible bouts of guilt. Their career had taken off, forcing them to tour most of the summer, leaving me home alone. And with the school year just beginning, it didn't look like that was going to change anytime soon. They offered to quit and get regular day jobs in order to stay home with me more, but I wouldn't hear of it. I was happy for them! After all, I was the one who needed to figure things out, not them.

Even after ending SOS and taking a break from Aiden (sort of), I still felt like I had more to learn about myself. Here it was, the start of my senior year, and I was completely stressed out and unable to focus. In fact, the only time I felt remotely like myself was when I was with Aiden—*working on our relationship.*

My yoga teacher had said that to really find my inner Tessa, I had to get away from everything, including cheerleading. She also told me that not-dating-but-still-dating Aiden was bad for my chi. I had promised to work on that. Maybe after this weekend.

"Time's up," I murmured, putting my hands on Aiden's shoulders as I gently pushed him off of me. "I have to meet Kira and the squad for practice."

"Why?" Aiden's kissable mouth frowned as he straightened up on the couch. "You're not a cheerleader anymore."

My back flinched again. I stood up, twisting from side to side, hoping it would help the tightness.

"I may not be a Smitten Kitten, Aiden, but Kira asked for my assistance. Homecoming is only a few weeks away, and, well, I'm a retired cheer expert. In fact, I had this spectacular routine—"

The phone rang. Pickles and ice cream! That was probably Kira wondering where I was. Even though I wasn't due at the gym for another half hour, I'd forgotten to call her back on Friday. And today was Sunday. Being with Aiden tended to make me lose track of time.

Careful not to further irritate my muscle, I slowly began to limp toward my phone.

"Shit, Tess. You really did hurt yourself," Aiden said as he helped me to the kitchen.

"I'm sure it's nothing." I waved him off, although each step sent white-hot splinters of pain down my leg. Once we reached the kitchen, Aiden let me go and walked to my fridge, opening it and ducking his head in. He was so cute when he rummaged for food.

I sighed, leaning up against the cool counter as I clicked on the phone. "Hello?"

"Tessa! Thank God you're home!" Leona said in a quick breath.

My heart sped up. "Everything okay?"

"No. Not even remotely. Kira's on the line too."

"Hey, Tess." Kira spoke up, sounding awful. She was captain of the Smitten Kittens; she wasn't allowed to sound glum.

"K," I said, completely concerned, "did something happen?" I really hoped this wasn't about her boyfriend. After she'd found out Darren had cheated on her last year, she'd finally rebounded this summer with a nice guy! She was overdue for some good karma. My pedicurist said so during our last session.

"I told Leona not to bother you," Kira said apologetically. "I have it under control."

"You *so* don't," Leona began. "Now zip it and let me bring Tessa up to speed."

Well, I was glad to hear that it didn't sound relationship related. Kira and Leona were probably arguing about proper skirt length again. I swear, if I didn't know those two had been friends since kindergarten, I'd think they hated each other. But I knew better. Smitten Kittens didn't hate. We were like sisters.

I tucked the phone into the crook of my neck and hobbled to the fridge, reaching above Aiden's bent-over frame to grab an ice pack from the freezer.

"I would have gotten that for you," he said, taking the pack from my hands to soften it up before handing it back. "You don't have to do everything yourself, Tess—like leading someone else's cheer practice." He intentionally said that last bit a little louder.

I narrowed my eyes at him, hoping that Kira and Leona hadn't heard. Aiden wasn't a big hit with the squad lately. They seemed to think that he was the reason for my sudden decrease in pep. But I denied it wholeheartedly. I was plenty peppy! Especially when Aiden was around.

Before walking away, I leaned in to give him a quick kiss on the lips and then put the ice to my back. I limped to the kitchen table, and when I sat down, Aiden motioned with his finger for me to come back over, but I shook my head and refocused on my phone call.

"Sorry, girls. What were we talking about?" I tried to turn in my chair so that I couldn't see Aiden anymore, but when I did, my muscle clenched again.

Butterscotch! I really hoped this wasn't a true pulled muscle, one that would require physical therapy. I had always been very careful about stretching before any athletic exertion. Maybe I was just getting old. After all, I would be eighteen this year.

"Have you even been listening?" Leona asked with a heavy sigh.

"I told you not to bug her," Kira said, as if I wasn't on the line. "Aiden's in town."

"Ugh," Leona moaned. "Doesn't that boy have his own place to live?"

My mouth twitched. I did not want to get into this discussion again. Sure, Aiden and I still spent a lot of quality time together, and yeah, I'd been a bit distant from the squad since I'd left, but that wasn't all because of my boyfriend...er...ex-boyfriend (sort of).

"Hurry," Aiden whispered as he walked past me, swishing my hair with his hand. "I have to get back to school pretty soon."

I watched Aiden stroll back into my living room, still shirtless in loose khakis, barefoot, handsome....

"Can I call you later?" I said absently into the phone. I didn't want Aiden to go back to college. Once he left, I knew it'd be at least a week—maybe two—before I saw him again.

I was just about to hang up when Leona's no-nonsense voice rang through my ears with urgency.

"Tessa," she snapped. "I'm calling you with a message. And it's from SOS."

SOS
CHANGE ORDER

Dear Clients,

Now that SOS has resumed its investigations, we want to clear up some confusion. We have created a fee schedule in addition to donations to keep our operation afloat. SOS is in need of new equipment, especially computer discs.

The new fee breakdown is as follows:

Cheater Report: $20

Potential Boyfriend Report: $15

Matchmaking Service: $15

Also, SOS will no longer be a secret organization. Details will soon follow, but rest assured, SOS will once again make this county a safer place for hearts.

Keep kicking ass.

SOS

SOS

Text: 555-1863

Exposing Cheaters for Over Three Years

CHAPTER TWO

MY. HEART. STOPPED.

"Leona, there is no SOS," I murmured, my face tingling. "We disbanded, remember? Even packed everything away in Izzie's grandparents' garage." I winced as I felt yet another twinge in my back. Just the letters *SOS* nearly brought on a panic attack.

I glanced into the living room, where Aiden was sitting on the couch, flipping through the television stations. He looked so peaceful. I hated thinking about SOS, especially when Aiden was here.

"I know," Leona said. "But it just came through on my SOS e-mail."

"Mine too," Kira chimed in.

"Check your account." Leona's voice was quickening—a sure sign of anxiety, which could trigger post-traumatic SOS disorder. Poor Kira had already gone to therapy to get rid of it once.

I limped toward my bedroom, holding up one finger to let Aiden know I'd be back in a minute. Leona was pretty tech savvy, but things like the Internet sometimes confused Kira. If this was all a misunderstanding, I wouldn't want to alarm Aiden for no reason.

But I could feel the stress clinging to me. My hairdresser had said that the drama of my junior year had worn all of the shine off my hair. I had to do weekly hot-oil treatments now. And hot oil was totally gross!

When I'd made Kira the new full-time captain of the Smitten Kittens, I'd told her she needed to act more dignified in uniform. She agreed.

And for the most part, the squad had understood my decision. Even Leona had thought a break would be good for me. Of course, she also thought that Kira would eventually mess up and that she could take over as captain. Her ambition was admirable.

So with all of that gone and Aiden usually away at college, it left me a bit on the lonely side. Which was why I spent all my extra money on *therapy*. Oprah once said that teenage girls needed to work on their self-esteem—put themselves first. I was taking her advice. I swear, that woman was brilliant.

I eased into the leather chair at my desk and flipped on the monitor. My room smelled like vanilla lavender, the perfect relaxation scent that my aromatherapist recommended. Matched with my freshly spruced-up pink walls and new comforter, I was swimming in positive feng shui.

"What's the subject line?" I asked into the phone. I didn't want to leave Aiden by himself too long, so I logged in and scanned the page. Goose bumps rose on my arms when I saw it. It couldn't be.

"It says, 'Now Taking New Clients,'" Leona answered.

"I see it," I whispered. The fruit salad I'd eaten for breakfast was about to make an encore appearance, but I swallowed hard and leaned toward the screen as I clicked the message.

"The squad is unhinged," Leona continued. "Kira is being completely unresponsive."

Kira gasped. "Did you ever think that I was launching an

investigation of my own, Leona? Tessa told us she was taking a break."

"But she can help! Tessa knows SOS better than anyone."

"I'm not going to argue," Kira said. "As captain, I'm in charge of the squad and SOS."

"There is no SOS," I mumbled, examining the page.

"Yeah," Leona started. "But maybe we should rethink that."

I closed my eyes. It was no secret that the Kittens were all itching to get back into the spying biz, but I'd put the brakes on it. I'd learned my lesson and hoped that they had too. "It's not up for discussion," I said, trying to sound authoritative, even though I had no real claim to the skirt anymore. "Now, are you sure none of the Smitten Kittens were involved in this SOS message?" I looked over the screen, trying to authenticate the letterhead. It was exactly the same as ours. The entire document was a perfect duplicate.

Kira cleared her throat. "I've spoken to the girls, and they've all insisted they're not involved. Although several of them suspect Chloe Ferril."

I rested my elbow on my desk, rubbing at my temple. "K, we need to have an internal investigation before we seek outside suspects."

"It's not us," Kira said. "And honestly, I can't believe you would even think that we'd go behind your back. I have enough problems now that you're gone. You didn't come to practice last week to teach us that cheer like you promised, and Izzie fell off the human pyramid and almost *died*!" I gasped.

"It's true," Leona added. "I had to call 9-1-1."

Kira sighed. "Tess, I know you're on a soul-searching mission or whatever, but we don't have time for internal investigations when our *spirit* is at stake! We don't even have our routine set for homecoming!"

"Are you serious?" I demanded. Homecoming wasn't far off, and it was a big deal for the school. We played the Ducks (our rivals), and the money raised was usually enough to buy our sports equipment for the year. But without a shiny new routine, we'd be a total disappointment.

"No offense, Kira," Leona said. "But the squad has fallen apart. Between your lifeless cheers and Izzie's new boyfriend, we're not connecting on any level."

"And what about you?" Kira shot back. "You've been taking electives in body shop. You show up at practice with grease on your skirt. Grease!"

I shook my head as feelings of guilt and regret rushed through me. Between therapies I had tried to sit in on as many practices as possible to help keep the transition smooth, but I had never really noticed how disjointed things had gotten. Sure, I knew there were problems the last time I'd seen their practice; their below-regulation-height herkies, for one. I just hadn't wanted to meddle.

"Girls," I said. "United front. Smitten Kittens don't hold animosity toward one another."

"Forget it," Kira said, sniffling. "I'm trying so hard, and no one appreciates it."

My heart broke. I hated that I'd done this to her. I'd completely overburdened her.

"Kira." Leona sighed. "Don't be overdramatic. I think you're a good captain. I just think that with this SOS problem, you're in over your head. We need Tessa's help."

I straightened my stiff back and adjusted the phone at my ear. "She's right, K. You are a good captain. And I gave you the squad because I trust you. You're the right leader for the Smitten Kittens."

Kira was quiet for a second. "Thanks," she said finally, sounding more courageous. "I know we'll pull the cheers together in time for the game."

"I know you will too. Now," I sighed. "Tell me about this SOS alert. I think it's important we figure out this mess before it gets out of hand. When was it sent?"

"This morning," Leona said, without missing a beat. "I got a call from Izzie at about nine. The message was sent to all the girls in the county—including us. Only these messages were sent to our old SOS accounts. She figured they must know—"

"Who we are," I finished, glancing back at the screen. My stomach twisted as I thought of how someone had found out our identities…and what they would do with them.

"But I guess it's not the first one," Leona added. "In the beginning of the summer they had sent out a flyer, just not to us. Wonder why we got one this time?"

"A warning?" Kira asked.

"Good guess," I said. It made total sense that whoever was sending out these messages would send one to us. Because really, it was their way of proving that they knew our identities. And a way to keep us quiet. Like a threat.

"So what's our move?" Leona asked. "Are we going to restart the real SOS?"

"No," I answered quickly, then clicked off the computer monitor and slowly got up from my desk chair. I had to think this through. Someone had discovered SOS, and even though I wasn't

captain anymore, I was still a Smitten Kitten at heart. I wasn't
going to let someone get away with pretending to be us. This was
a forgery of the worst kind—a reputation hijack.

"Listen up, girls," I said. "Call the rest of the squad and
schedule an emergency meeting for tomorrow morning. I'd like to
open an investigation of my own."

When I came into the living room, Aiden was sprawled across the
sofa, looking completely bored.

"What was that about?" he asked. "Kira have another dating
disaster?"

I walked around the couch and flopped down against his legs.
"No," I said, not wanting to bring up SOS yet. "Kira doesn't have
anymore DDs. She's settled down."

Aiden widened his eyes. "Seriously? Kira's got a man?"

"I told you," I said, running my hand down Aiden's calf as I
leaned on him. "That guy she met over the summer."

"I don't remember."

"They're totally steady. Heard he's really nice, too. Not like
her usual."

"Huh." Aiden considered this. "Well, good for her. I felt bad
after the whole Darren thing."

"Me too."

I pulled a peach-flavored Jolly Rancher out of my pocket and
began crunching it between my teeth. I was stalling. I knew that I
had to tell Aiden about the faux SOS, but I was nervous. We'd had
such a nice weekend, and bringing up the super-secret snooping
society that I'd once used to spy on him might ruin the mood. I
was torn. "So..."

"Uh-oh. What?" Aiden rested his elbows on his knees as he stared at me intently. It made my throat tighten.

"Something...happened," I said.

"Wait, what? Are you okay?" Aiden reached out to touch my hand protectively. It made my mouth twitch into a smile. I hadn't felt all that protected lately.

I exhaled and closed my eyes. "Today every girl in Redmond received a solicitation from SOS."

Aiden cleared his throat and pulled his hand away. When I looked at him, his jaw was clenched. I'd promised him that my spying days were behind me.

"But I didn't do it!" I said quickly, knowing that SOS was still a sore subject with us. "It was a fake communication. I didn't send it!"

"A solicitation? And none of the Sex Kittens wrote it?" Aiden asked, sounding suspicious. "It said SOS, right?"

I shook my head, feeling a little annoyed. "It's *Smitten* Kittens. And yes, it said SOS, but none of them were involved."

"But the Smitten Kittens are the only ones that know how to pull off stuff like that, right? Didn't you keep the files?"

I furrowed my brow, surprised that Aiden would mention our files. Thing was, Leona had asked to convert all of our paper forms into electronic ones last year. But since Kira had trouble figuring out how to open the documents, we'd kept both. I'd never talked about the SOS system with Aiden, so it seemed an odd thing to bring up.

"No," I said slowly, shaking my head. "We stored the files somewhere safe."

Aiden stared down at the wood floor of my living room. "Well,

I don't know what to say, Tess. My money would be on a rogue Kitten. But if you're sure…"

"No," I said. "Kira was over ninety percent sure that it wasn't anyone on the squad. And it definitely wasn't me. I trust the squad. They wouldn't do this." Aiden shrugged and I pursed my lips, looking him over. He knew about the SOS files. In fact, Aiden knew about *a lot* of things. "Hey, you…you didn't mention SOS to anyone, did you?" Like maybe Chloe Ferril?

My ex-boyfriend spun to face me so quickly that I nearly choked.

"Me?" he asked, his mouth hanging open. "You think I ratted you out to the school?" He laughed. "Oh, baby," he said, taking my hand again. "If I was going to spill your secrets, I'd make sure to blackmail you first." He grinned wickedly.

I couldn't help but smile as I wondered what exactly he'd want as payment. Aiden's hand was warm on mine. I loved that feeling— that safe feeling. He looked over, but I saw his expression change as he ran his thumb over my hand. Aiden was thinking, and that was never a good sign.

"Hey," I said, realizing that I'd just brought up the one thing that still hurt him. "I promised you that SOS would stop spying, and we did. I wouldn't lie to you again."

Aiden brought his fingers to my cheek, touching it softly. "I believe you," he whispered. "I just…I don't want you getting yourself into trouble again." He leaned over to give me a quick kiss.

"Okay."

He sighed, smiling a little. "Now what did this fake Kitty have to say?"

I felt better. Aiden believed me and he was looking out for me.

He was my guy, even if technically he wasn't really. "Well," I began, "I only saw the one e-mail. No word yet if it went beyond that, but we have an emergency meeting scheduled for tomorrow."

"Meeting?" Aiden glanced at me. "You're not thinking of restarting SOS, are you?"

I shook my head. "No. But the squad needs to meet to discuss this. Aiden, e-mails are going out with the SOS logo on them. Someone who knows us is a total copy-Kitten! And I need to find out who it is."

"*Copy-Kitten?* Oh, baby, you're so cute."

"This is not a time for cute!"

"Okay, okay. I'm sorry. What can I do to help you?" he asked, his voice getting softer, as if he knew it would turn me into pistachio pudding.

I chewed on the corner of my lip. Surely with his ties to the boys at our school, Aiden would be privy to information I couldn't get on my own.

"I need you to call Darren and some of the other guys from the team. See if they know about any funny business going on at school. But be careful not to out us. We don't need anyone else knowing about SOS or that we've been heading it for the last few years."

Aiden sighed again. "Tess, I haven't talked to Darren in weeks. I'm not on the team anymore. I don't even go to your school. Don't you think it would look weird if I called him now?"

"Not if you play it smooth."

He grinned. "Oh, I'm always smooth."

"Are you going to call Darren or not?" But he was right. He was always smooth.

"Fine," he said, sounding sort of annoyed. "I'll call and check into it. But I guarantee they don't know anything. If they did—" He stopped. Aiden knew the ramifications of our exposure. It might involve mobs with pitchforks.

"Thanks," I whispered.

"Anytime. I've got to go," he murmured, leaning down to kiss the top of my head. "I have to hit the gym, and I have class early in the morning."

I frowned. "Will you call me later?" I asked, not wanting to move away from him. I knew I was being clingy, but I almost couldn't help myself. With things so different between us, I felt like I had to fight for every second with him.

Aiden paused, making my stomach twist in pretzel knots. "I'll try," he said. "But I have…plans tonight."

"Oh." Did he have a date? I pressed my lips together, trying to remind myself that ex-boyfriends were allowed to date. Especially when their ex-girlfriends spied, lied, and cheated on them. But then I reminded myself that ex-boyfriends who slept over at my house were absolutely not allowed to date anyone. Except me. The rules of ex-dating still had me all turned around.

"Let go, Tess," Aiden said, pulling out of my grasp. Then his eyes weakened. "It's not anything like that," he whispered. "I just have to get in a workout, and then I'm meeting a few friends for dinner. That's all. Don't look so sad. You know I can't stand it when you're sad."

"I know." I tried to sound as perky as possible. Still there was an ache in my chest, a dull one, but it was there. I tried to smile. "Call me tomorrow, okay?"

"Course, baby," he said, moving to kiss me deeply. When he

pulled away, I felt a bit calmer. But only a bit.

I watched from my seat as he walked around gathering his stuff, never glancing at me. In fact, it seemed like he was trying not to.

Before heading for the door, Aiden moved in front of me. "You know how much I care about you, right, Tess?" he asked softly.

I nodded, reaching up to put my hands on either side of his face. I kissed him, wanting to keep him here, knowing I couldn't. When I pulled away, his eyes were closed.

"I'll call you soon," he said. And then he walked away.

"I love you," I called, but the door was already closed.

Alone, I covered my face with my palms. *Deep breath.* I needed to stay focused. There was a copy-Kitten out there, and they'd already inflicted serious damage.

For the love of unicorns! This was quite a mess—one that I'd have to rein in.

It was time for some serious sherlocking.

ASSIGNMENT 2

9:00 P.M., SEPTEMBER 13

The operative glanced toward her rearview mirror and slicked on a deadly shade of Midnight Red lipstick. A serious mission like this required serious color. Tate Donovan had appeared on the Naughty List, but his accomplice was unnamed. And even though Tate was single, the addition of his name meant that the accomplice was not. The anonymous texts were really coming in fast now that SOS had been restarted.

The operative smoothed her lips together and smiled. This would be easy. Tate was idling just a few cars away in his black Ford F-250, waiting for his order at the McDonald's drive-through window. He had someone in the passenger seat—a girl—but the thick tint of his windows obscured her face.

As the truck pulled away from the window, immediately heading for the exit, the operative swung her car out of line to follow him into the street. Damn it. She really wanted some french fries.

She stayed far enough back to keep her face hidden from view in his mirror. After a few turns, the operative realized that Tate wasn't heading to his home in the exclusive Redmond Hills. She narrowed her eyes and pressed on the accelerator. The operative was glad to see that *this* cheat was going according to plan. She'd beat Tessa's record yet.

Minutes later, they arrived in a downtown neighborhood. One with small, wood-paneled homes tucked close to one another. The yards were unkempt, overgrown with weeds. Tate's truck slowed and eventually stopped in front of a green, one-story house. He cut his engine.

The operative clicked off her lights and turned into a driveway several houses down from the suspect's vehicle. Quickly she snapped her zoom lens on her camera. She rolled down the window just an inch and pointed the slim viewfinder at the truck, eager to catch the accomplice's identity.

She could see only a vague silhouette as the couple turned to face each other. The operative held her breath, her adrenaline pumping at the thought of the impending cheat. It would be her first catch. Stupid tinted windows.

Every so often, the operative could make out Tate's arm as he reached out for the girl, but the girl pushed it away several times. The operative pulled back from the camera, confused.

Just then, the driver's door opened and Tate stepped out. He looked nice. His chin-length, chestnut hair was pulled back into a ponytail, and he was wearing jeans and a pale pink sweater with a colored shirt underneath. The operative smiled at this. Only a really secure guy wore pink.

When he reached the passenger door, Tate glanced over one shoulder. The operative quickly dodged down, unsure whether she'd been spotted. She all of a sudden wished she'd parked farther away. Shit. She would need to be more careful.

Slowly she poked her head up just enough to catch a glimpse

of Tate closing the passenger door, his arm draped protectively across the back of a female with a short brown bob. They had already begun walking toward the house when Tate leaned down to kiss the top of her head tenderly.

The operative felt a little flutter in her stomach. Did cheaters have hearts? She dismissed the thought and lifted her camera to zoom in, tense with the need to capture the girl's face on film.

"Move," the operative muttered, trying to see around Tate's pink sweater. She brought her left thumb to her mouth and chewed on the nail nervously, flaking off the polish before she caught herself. Tessa would never walk around so unkempt. The operative burned with resentment.

Tate stepped back from his accomplice. Then, after a quick embrace, he turned and left her on her doorstep. The operative clicked the picture and gasped, straightening up.

"Jenn," she whispered. The case had just gotten more complicated.

CHAPTER THREE

"TESSA!" IZZIE YELLED THE MINUTE I STEPPED INTO the gymnasium. She jumped up from the bleacher and clapped happily. Her red hair bounced over her shoulders, somehow adding even more sparkle to her look. I noticed that her cheer skirt was well above regulation length, showing off her muscular thighs. But I wasn't captain anymore. I needed to keep my advice to myself.

"Thank goodness you're here," she said, green eyes brimming with tears. "We've missed you."

I furrowed my brow as I crossed the wooden planks of the gym floor to center court. "Izzie, we went out together for pizza Thursday night." It seemed that out of the skirt, I was invisible.

She wrinkled her nose. "Tess, that was two weeks ago."

I stared at her, confused. Had it been that long?

"Told you she'd be here," Leona called to Izzie from across the court. She was sitting back, leaning against the bleacher in a well-worn skirt—one with the hem fraying at the edges. "Hey," she said to me in greeting, popping her gum loudly.

"Uh, *hey*." She wasn't wearing her glasses, which seemed a bit odd. She hated contacts. And I could see why Kira had been so concerned about Leona taking body shop. She had the tiniest smudge of what looked like grease on her cheek. "Can I have a word?" I asked her.

Leona rolled her eyes, blowing her dark bangs away from her face. "Sure," she mumbled, making her way toward me.

Kira hadn't arrived yet, and even though I didn't want to step on her sneakers, I knew that Leona was a tough nut to crack. I thought that maybe I could talk to her in private and ratchet down the animosity factor. It didn't help that she and Kira consistently got under each other's skin. They fought like an old married couple. But not in the adorable-old-people way.

"Glad you're here, Tess. We really need you to step up," Leona said, looking relieved.

"Of course." I put my hands at my hips. "Now, what's going on with you? Let's talk." It was going to be a challenge to give advice out of uniform. I almost felt like an imposter. Also, I was so overwhelmed by my own problems that I wasn't sure I could solve Leona's too. And by the poorly combined eyeliner-and-shadow combo, it was obvious she had one.

Leona stopped chewing her gum and measured me with her dark eyes. "Talk about what?"

"What's up with this body-shop nonsense? I don't know, Leona. I think it's sweet that you're cultivating your knowledge about engines and oil changes, but getting dirty? It doesn't make sense."

Leona sighed and twirled the ends of her dark hair in one hand. "It's not about the cars," she said quietly, looking up once to make sure no one was listening. "There's...a guy."

I gasped. In as long as I'd known her, Leona had shown little interest in the opposite sex, other than busting them as they got their grooves on with people other than their girlfriends.

"Who?" I asked, now completely fascinated.

She exhaled, her breath smelling like the watermelon Jolly

Rancher she was always sucking on. "His name is Marco Sandoval. He's a junior."

I tried to remember if we'd ever been called on assignment over Marco. Nothing came to mind. At least there was that. So few innocents were left! "Is he nice?"

"Yeah," Leona mumbled. "Really nice. And he's smart. Maybe even smarter than I am."

I smiled. That was highly improbable. "So what does that have to do with you taking body shop?"

"Because that's where he always is. His dad runs Sandoval's Repair, and Marco is planning on taking over the business after graduation, so he has a fast track in auto-body shop."

I tilted my head, still not understanding why Leona had to go to this much trouble over a guy. She was pretty, smart, and well-accessorized (normally). "Why don't you just ask him out—or better yet, tell him to ask you out?" I was a modern Kitten. No need to wait on a boy these days. Well, except for Aiden. But that was different. We had history.

Suddenly Leona's normally level stare faltered. "Because I don't think he likes me."

"What? Why in the world wouldn't he?" I was genuinely surprised.

Leona looked at the wood floor and kicked at it with her sneaker. "Remember that time I got into an argument at the pool with Lucy McGill?"

"When you called her fat?" I cringed as I spoke. I hated to think that Leona could be so harsh, even if Lucy did accidentally-on-purpose dump her root beer float in Leona's lap just because she didn't like cheerleaders. Another classic case of cheerleader envy. It was an epidemic, really.

Leona looked embarrassed. "Yeah, that time. Anyway, she's Marco's cousin, and he heard about it. He thinks I was totally unprovoked. He told me that he couldn't hang out with someone who's shallow." A tear started to run down her cheek, but she rubbed it away. "And I'm not shallow," she whispered harshly.

I chewed on the corner of my bottom lip. "So you joined body shop and started getting dirty," I said for her.

"I wanted to prove that I wasn't as one-dimensional as he thought. And Tessa, I think it's working. But…"

She paused, and I was afraid she was going to break into total hysterics. I reached over to pat her shoulder supportively. I should have known about this sooner.

Leona sniffled and straightened her posture. "It's awful," she whispered. "I haven't worn a headband or earrings in three weeks. Three. Weeks."

"No!" That *was* awful. Even though my own love life was completely convoluted, I couldn't stand the thought of Leona changing herself to get someone to like her. I mean, had Marco *seen* her accessories collection? It was fabulous.

Just then, the gymnasium door popped open and Kira flittered in, her blonde curls framing her face as she flashed a brave smile, trying to look captain-like. "Sorry I'm late," she called to the squad. "But I have news."

Leona made a barfing sound, and when I glared at her, she rolled her eyes. "I hate when she does the power-trip thing," Leona leaned over to whisper. "Hey, don't say anything about Marco, okay, Tess? I don't want it getting back to him."

I nodded, but I had a small pang in my chest. I needed to help her. Once I sorted out this copy-Kitten mess, Leona was top priority. Well, that and working off the extra five pounds I'd put on since I'd stopped cheering. My skinny jeans were seriously starting to cut off the circulation to my ankles.

"Oh, good!" Kira said, noticing me in center court. "You're here already." She jogged over, sneakers squeaking, and hugged me. "Oh, thank God, Tessa," she murmured in my ear as we embraced. "I've got nothing, and they're turning on me. I'm so royally nailed without you."

"I think it's screwed," I said as I pulled back to look at her.

"That too." Kira forced a smile and then spun back to the squad. "I just checked my e-mail, and it seems another report has gone out. The fake SOS is not only charging money for their services; they're taking the organization public."

Izzie gasped. "Our reputations will be destroyed."

"Take a breath, Iz," Kira said. "I think they're only taking the spying public and not the members." She shot a side glance to me before continuing. "Luckily for us, Tessa's here now, and together we're going to fix this."

I was pretty sure I had no idea how to help fix it, but I nodded and stepped up next to Kira, facing the squad. It was good to look unified.

Kira rubbed her lips together as if deep in thought. "We have a fraud," she announced. "And after discussing it with Tessa, I ran a thorough check last night and have determined that none of the Kittens were involved."

"Well, of course we weren't," Leona snapped.

"Right, Leona," Kira responded. "Like you hadn't considered continuing SOS."

Leona reset her jaw. "No more than you, *Kira*."

"Enough," I said, holding up my hands. "Look, I made some calls, and that SOS notice went out to every girl in Washington

High, West Washington, and Fairfield. But as far as Google Search is concerned, we're still very much secret. The copy-Kitten could be bluffing."

"What if she's not?" Izzie yelled, her voice cracking. "If the copy-Kitten exposes us to everyone, the boys at school will be totally ticked!"

"Shit. She's right," Leona muttered from her spot on the bleachers. I shot her a dirty look, but she just shrugged. Actually, I echoed her sentiment internally, just in a much more polite way.

The entire squad began fretting, and I knew I had to take control. Kira was right. They were turning on her. I stepped forward.

"Listen," I said. "I'm hoping that the girls we've protected will be able to see that this is an obvious forgery. *Most* of us"—I eyed Leona—"don't cuss. And hopefully that, coupled with the fact that they're charging money, will jump out as phony-baloney nonsense so that even if they do name us, no one will buy it. I have no idea what this copy-Kitten wants, but our priority should be finding the culprit and stomping her out before she can do something we'll all regret."

"Should I type up a rebuttal?" Leona asked. "Calling out the imposter?"

I sighed. "Unfortunately, I don't think we can. The copy-Kitten has our identities in her back pocket. We can't go on offense until we know more." I glanced down at the floor, noticing how my white sneakers covered up my toes—the toes that used to always be painted (badly). Now they were colorless.

"We need to set up surveillance," I said quietly. "Starting with Chloe Ferril." My stomach sank. I knew this would directly violate the promise I'd made to Aiden. Sure, technically I wasn't restarting SOS, but it was still spying.

"You should do it." Kira pointed, volunteering me as she smiled. "After all, Tess, you still owe her a little payback for the alarm clock incident." She tapped her forehead with her index finger.

"Good point," I replied. I wouldn't mind catching the ex-vixen who tried to steal my ex-boyfriend (sort of). I turned to the squad, and as they looked back at me so attentively, I sighed. I wanted to do something more to help out my best friend. "Girls," I pleaded. "While I check into Chloe, I need you all to do something for me. Kira's been working really hard to get you prepped for homecoming. Can you please show her some more respect? This routine is our most important of the year."

Kira let out a breathy noise next to me, and I felt her move closer. The squad looked around at each other guiltily and then nodded toward us, mumbling apologies to Kira. Well, except for Leona. She was picking at her nails.

"Great! Now go kick some tail!" I added, hoping to rev them up before practice. As they began to adjust their waistbands and hair ties, Kira leaned her shoulder into mine.

"Thanks, Tess," she whispered. "Your support means a lot." When I looked over to her, Kira's blue eyes were brimming with tears, and I realized I'd missed the snot out of her. And the squad.

SOS
CHANGE-OF-STATUS MEMO

CASE: 002
CLIENT: Jenn Duarte

Jenn Duarte originally contacted SOS about her boyfriend Riley Richards's relationship with an unnamed female. The female was later identified as Megan Wright, her best friend. Although the cheating has not been confirmed, there is cause to continue the investigation.

However, the client has since been named a subject in another case. Ms. Duarte was observed with Tate Donovan, who is not her boyfriend.

This may be a case of mistaken identity or a double cheat. Right now, both Ms. Duarte and Mr. Richards are official suspects.

The investigation will resume immediately.

SOS

Text: 555-1863
Exposing Cheaters for Over Three Years

CHAPTER FOUR

KIRA SLAPPED HER HANDS TOGETHER TO SIGNAL the start of practice, her loud clap echoing through the gymnasium. Just then, a cell phone sounded from the bleachers—it had a techno ring tone. I tsked and looked sideways at her. I'd never allowed the girls to have their phones on in the gymnasium.

"That's me," Leona called, leaning over to dig through her backpack. "I had my tech guy trace the SOS e-mail to get an IP address."

"Oh, well, good thinking," I said, truly impressed. Leona was a better spy than even I had realized.

"Hello?" she said. "Uh-huh. Uh-huh. Yep. Wait, *what?*" Leona's eyes snapped up to mine.

"What is it?" I asked, my heart beginning to pound in my chest.

Leona continued to stare at me as she nodded, as if the guy on the other end of the line could see her. "Thanks, Greg," she said absently into the phone. "I'm sure I can track down the rest of the information on my own. Talk to you later." Leona lowered the phone to her lap and snapped it shut.

I could feel Kira standing there, swinging her head to look between Leona and me. "For Pete's sake! What is going on?" she squeaked.

"What's the IP address?" I asked, my voice near a whisper. Leona's expression reminded me of that day when we'd gotten the fake cheater report on Aiden. Oh, no. Leona had bad news—one-hundred percent.

"He said…" She paused and furrowed her brow. "He said that the SOS e-mail was linked to one of our accounts." Kira reached out to take my arm, steadying herself.

"What?" I asked, Kira's hands like ice on my skin. "Whose account was it?"

Leona looked down at the phone in her lap, then back up to meet my eyes, swallowing hard. "He said the e-mail came from *your* computer, Tess. That means…" She faltered. "The copy-Kitten has been in your house."

Hot fudge sundae! With nuts.

This was not good. I touched my hand to my chest and gasped for breath. Someone had been on my computer. Someone had been in my house!

"I need to sit down," I said, stumbling toward the bleachers, my sneakers squeaking on the wood floor. My entire world felt tilted.

The girls surrounded me, holding my arms as I sat down. Once there, Leona reached over to pat my thigh. "Hopefully they didn't take pictures of you while you were sleeping or anything," she said supportively.

"Leona!" Kira snapped.

"What?" she asked, holding up her hands. "I said *hopefully*."

My brain was spinning like a pinwheel. Who would have had the nerve to break into my house? I closed my eyes. It was sort of like, how did I have the nerve to break into the houses of cheaters so many times? Could this be karma?

Leona tapped her shoe. "Tessa, you sure you didn't know about the e-mails? I mean, they did come from your computer."

She sounded completely suspicious! I couldn't believe she'd ask me that. "No! Of course not."

"You have been different lately, Tess," Izzie agreed. "Maybe you have PTSOSD."

"I don't have post-traumatic SOS disorder! Girls, I promise you. I had nothing to do with this."

"I believe her," Kira said loudly. "I checked everyone's phone records and social calendars against the dates of the e-mails. As far as I can tell, none of us could have done it."

I exhaled. At least Kira was making sense.

"Sorry," Izzie apologized to me. "I guess I'm just a little paranoid."

"We all are," Leona added.

Suddenly the muscle spasm struck again and I groaned, clutching my lower back.

"Oh, no!" Izzie screamed, nearly falling on top of me. "She's having a seizure! Does anyone know CPR?"

"Stop," I tried to say over the frantic squeals of the squad. "I'm fine, girls. Really. It's just a muscle spasm."

"Do you want us to call a chiropractor?" Izzie asked, her eyes wide with concern. I couldn't help but think she felt a little guilty for accusing me of being the copy-Kitten.

"No. I'll be okay."

"You sure?" Kira asked me, pushing Izzie aside to squat down in front of me.

I nodded to her, but I could tell by her dimple-free expression that she knew how scared I was.

"I'm freaking out a little," I whispered, glancing around the room. "Who knew our names?"

Kira shook her head, her hair swishing over her shoulders. "I don't know. But I think we need to think about homecoming. And what we want to—"

"It's totally Chloe," Leona announced, snapping her gum. "That bitch is crazy. Always has been. I mean, she threw a clock at your head! This wouldn't be too far off."

"Very true," Kira echoed. "It could be Chloe. But Tessa has already agreed to investigate her while we get ready for the game. We don't want to screw up the plan."

"Kira's right," I said, trying to stretch out my back. "And besides, I promised Aiden that SOS was over and—"

"Here we go," Leona mumbled, turning away.

"What?" Her tone bothered me.

Leona groaned. "*Aiden.* Don't take this the wrong way, but our lives do not revolve around the promises you made to your ex-boyfriend."

My eyes stung, but I blinked quickly, brushing off her comment. "Keep things in perspective, Leona," I said. "SOS didn't do any of us any good, and reviving it now would be a horrible way to start the senior year."

"Well, *somebody* doesn't agree," Kira said under her breath, beginning to bite at the skin around her thumbnail. Then she gasped and looked up. "Wait! What if the copy-Kitten is a guy? Could it be Christian?"

Just the mention of his name buried me in guilt. "He wouldn't," I said. "He hasn't said a word to me yet this year. I haven't even seen him since he started taking classes at Redmond Community College. Besides, I think he learned his lesson. Especially after

Aiden punched him in the face at playoffs last year."

"Right." Izzie giggled. "He totally coldcocked him."

"Cold *what*?" Kira asked, spinning around to look at her.

"Oh my God, you two!" Leona snapped. "Stay on topic. Tessa has been violated!"

"Don't make it sound so graphic," I murmured. But that was exactly how I felt. My mouth was drying up from the anxiety. "Do you have any gum?" I asked.

Kira gasped. "You…you never chew gum. You said it was disrespectful to the skirt!"

"Well," I replied, taking a piece that Leona held out. "I don't wear the uniform anymore." I popped it in my mouth, the berry blast of it sweetening my breath. "And besides, this is unlike any problem we've faced before. We're not falling off of roofs, K. Someone was in my room! Someone's been watching me!"

My eyes became blurry with tears, but I didn't have enough time to blink them away. Before the first tear dripped down, my squad huddled around, promising to high kick anyone that came close to me.

I felt sacked. Someone had figured us out, stolen our files, and sent e-mails from *my* computer. That meant they knew everything. About Mary Rudick and our beginning. About last year with Chloe and Aiden. Maybe even about Christian and me. They could expose us at any moment.

I'd worked hard to put that part of my life behind me. I'd seen countless therapists. Well, beauticians. But now, it was like the wound was fresh. And without the power of the skirt, I wasn't sure I could cheer us through this latest drama. Right about now, I wasn't even sure I could cheer us out of a paper bag.

The first warning bell rang. "Dang it!" Kira said, promptly unhugging me. "We just blew our practice. *And* I was supposed to meet Joel before class."

I sniffled, wiping at my cheeks as I looked up at her. "Doesn't he usually meet you before lunch?" I'd only met Kira's boyfriend a handful of times since they usually left campus for lunch, but I was completely supportive of their courtship. He didn't have tattoos or a rap sheet.

Kira ran her red-polished finger across her lips, smoothing out her gloss. "Uh-huh. But we were going to have a talk before class, something about space." She looked up at the ceiling. "Maybe astronauts or something? I don't know. Anyway, I'll catch you up on it later. But call me as soon as the surveillance is set on Chloe, okay?" Kira didn't wait for an answer before she winked and turned to dash toward the gymnasium's double doors.

"Sure," I murmured, although she was gone before I had the chance.

"I have to go too, Tess," Leona said, climbing up off the bleacher and combing through her bangs with her fingers. She looked down at me as if I were a scared child. I felt like one. "Don't stress," she said. "We've got your back."

"Thanks." As I watched her and the rest of the squad leave, Izzie came to sit next to me. I exhaled and looked sideways at her. She grinned.

"We can ditch?" she said, her green eyes sparkling with a devious plan surely involving the mall and her grandma's credit card. "I have Sam's car today."

Sam, her college-age boyfriend, let her keep his car every

Monday, Wednesday, and Friday while he had classes on the community-college campus. He was a total keeper. Long sandy hair, light eyes. Yeah, Izzie scored an A-plus with him.

"Can't go," I said, after considering it. "I have a test in language arts this period."

She sighed. "I should probably stay too. We're having gym out in the field today. At least it's soccer." She beamed. Izzie had been one of the best forwards on Washington High's soccer team for the past three years. It was totally her calling. Well, besides cheerleading. "Do you want me to walk with you to class?" she asked, looking worried. She was such a doll—porcelain, not Barbie.

"It's okay," I said, touching her arm. "I don't want you to be late. I'll catch up with you at lunch, though?"

Izzie nodded before turning to jog across the wood floor. When she was gone, I flopped back down on the bleacher and brought my knees to my chest, hugging my legs. Right now, language arts was the least of my concerns. I was…confused.

Someone knew about us. But who? Methodically, I ran down the line of every cheat we'd ever caught, every awkward moment I'd ever had, every—

Suddenly I realized that I was completely alone in the gymnasium. The overhead lights buzzed, and I darted an uncomfortable glance around the empty room. I swallowed hard, listening and scanning the court. There was no one here, but I felt like I was being watched.

"Hello?" I called out, painfully aware that this was exactly how every horror movie started out. I let go of my legs and struggled to stand up. The pain in my back was returning with poorly timed vengeance. The room was silent.

Then I heard it. From the locker room there was a loud banging sound. Crab cakes! I spun, walking quickly to the double doors, becoming more and more paranoid with each step. I broke into a run. My heart was pumping, and my blood flowed to my face as the feeling of being chased crawled over my skin. I wanted to yell for Izzie, but she was long gone by now.

When I got to the heavy metal door, I ran against it, pushing it open as hard as I could. And screamed.

"Ah!" Joel Fletcher screamed back. He was just outside the doorway, standing in the hall, clutching his chest. "What the hell, Tessa?" he said, bending over to take a deep breath as he rested his palms on his knees. "You nearly killed me with the door."

I was still gasping, staring at him. When he wasn't doubled over in fear, Kira's boyfriend was quite a catch. He had short, messy-but-cute brown hair, big hazel eyes, and a killer T-shirt collection. "Sorry," I said absently, letting the door close behind me with a clank. My mind was fuzzy from the adrenaline rush.

He raised his head to look at me, exhaling loudly. "I didn't mean to freak out. I was just coming to find Kira and—"

"She went looking for you. She said you guys were going to talk about outer space." Which—in my opinion—was a weird conversation. But I didn't judge. My ex-boyfriend (sort of) was into toes.

Joel stepped back and laughed, shaking his head. He smiled, his lips revealing one slightly crooked tooth. It was adorable. "Like, astronauts outer space?" he asked.

I nodded, glancing behind him into the crowded hallway. I must have looked distressed because Joel reached out to touch my hand. I quickly yanked it away, thrown off by the contact.

He apologized. "I'm so sorry! I didn't mean...I...Are

you okay?" His eyebrows were pulled together; he seemed concerned. I felt bad for acting like a spaz, but I couldn't shake my anxiety.

"No," I said, then paused. "I mean, yes, I'm fine. Thank you for asking. And again, sorry for almost hitting you with the door."

Joel watched me. "Eh, no big deal." He shrugged. "A broken nose would have added character." He grinned at me, setting me at ease again. Something about him was just nice. He hadn't meant anything by the hand touch. I was just on edge. I sighed.

"Are you heading down the English hallway?" I asked, motioning in that direction.

"Uh…sure."

I couldn't remember where Kira's first class was, but I knew it wasn't in that direction. Still, I was just happy for any company after my self-induced scare.

The crowded hallways had nearly emptied by the time we started walking. I was going to be totally tardy, but in light of all the drama that just went down, I didn't mind. At least in detention I couldn't be stalked. Wait. Could I?

"Can I ask you something?" Joel said, turning to look at me.

"Of course." It was so polite of him to check!

"What exactly did Kira tell you she and I were meeting about? I'm pretty sure I'm not going to space camp anytime soon."

"She said it was something about space." I paused, just realizing how silly that sounded. Why would Joel want to talk about outer— "Oh," I held up one finger. "You meant…*space*, space?" I gasped. "Joel? Are you breaking up with her?" My heart nearly leapt from my chest. He couldn't break up with Kira—they were perfect together.

"No!" Joel put his hand on my bare upper arm, warming my skin.

"Oh."

"Definitely not."

"Sorry I—"

"It's just—"

"Sorry. Go ahead—"

"You talk—"

I reached up to cover his mouth with my hand. Just then, the late bell rang and I paused, my palm slightly damp from the wetness of his mouth.

"Mm hm mm hm mmmm," he said, tickling my fingers.

I scrunched my nose. "What?"

Joel pointed to my hand. I widened my eyes and dropped my arm. "Sorry!"

When I wiped my palm on my jeans, he smiled. "I said you can probably take your hand off my mouth now."

"Right."

"Yep."

Joel and I faced each other, late for class. The sleeve of his black vintage Aerosmith T-shirt was folded slightly where it met his bicep, and I had to fight the urge to smooth it out. Instead I pressed my lips together in a smile.

"For the record," Joel said quietly. "I was meeting Kira to ask if she wanted some space. Not *outer* space." He shrugged. "She hasn't been around much lately. She calls it 'captain stress.'"

A potent combination of guilt and sadness filled me. I hated to think of Kira becoming distraught over cheerleading. Cheerleading was meant to embody positivity and school spirit. To feel stressed over it was completely tragic.

"I'm sure she doesn't want space," I confided, leaning close enough to Joel to bump his shoulder encouragingly with my own. "It's probably just because homecoming is in a few weeks. Things will get back to normal soon." I hoped I looked more convincing than I felt.

He studied me. "You're probably right."

"*Right?* I definitely haven't heard that in a while."

Joel gave me a strange look, as though he was about to say something. Instead, he just smiled. "I'll see you around, Tess." He turned to walk back the way we'd come.

"Nice talking with you," I called after him. Then I watched as he rounded the corner, leaving me alone in the hallway.

ASSIGNMENT 2

1:00 A.M., SEPTEMBER 15

The operative drove aimlessly around the city, thinking about Jenn's case. Something wasn't sitting right. The operative hadn't gotten proof of either suspect actually cheating, but she was sure that whatever they were up to wasn't so innocent. Did the original SOS have problems like this? Weren't all cheats one-hundred percent?

Snapping back to reality, the operative realized where she'd inadvertently taken herself. She pulled to the side of the road and shifted into park, killing the engine. Unease filled her chest, and she began to tap her dark nails on the steering wheel, constructing a plan.

She had to give Tessa credit: organizing an entire fleet of spies took a lot of work and dedication. But she knew she could do it better, especially since Tessa was distracted with Aiden. Her relationship blunder had left open the perfect opportunity for the operative to take SOS from her—and do it right.

The operative looked out the driver's window to the quaint little house across the street, its bedroom light still on despite the hour. She'd slipped in there weeks ago, slowly gathering all the templates from Tessa's computer in order to take over SOS. She'd sent out e-mails—some on a time delay—and then found her way to Izzie's grandparents' garage for the equipment.

The cell phone on the passenger seat vibrated. The operative snatched it up and scrolled through the message. Her alert had gone off, retrieving all of Riley's texts from the past two weeks. It was good, since the listening device she'd planted under his desk hadn't worked. She wondered if her lipstick had deactivated it. Her heart pounded as she waited to see what she'd find on her phone. She needed something.

"I love you, M."

The operative's red lips parted as she hitched in a breath. She waited for a response, and when nothing registered, she felt a bit of sadness touch her. She'd known what it was like to love someone and have it not returned. In a way, she felt bad for Riley.

The operative turned again to look at Tessa's house, unsure why she was even here.

She had an assignment. One she was determined to finish.

The operative started her car, glancing once more out the window. Then she saw her. Tessa Crimson standing in front of her full-length mirror—in her cheerleading uniform. The operative's mouth opened. Tessa wasn't even on the squad anymore, but…she wore her cheer uniform at home? Something about this little secret both pleased and irritated the operative. It was sad—pathetic almost—and it made her feel sorry for Tessa. And that wouldn't do. Tessa had already lost Aiden, the squad, and SOS. Now the operative just needed to make sure things stayed that way. It was the only way to achieve her goal.

Shifting gears, she swung out into the road, illuminating her interior with the streetlights, and headed for home.

The cheaters would be caught. She'd make sure of it.

CHAPTER FIVE

THERE WERE WHISPERS. SINCE SCHOOL HAD started last month, there had been lots of gossip about Aiden and me—about why we broke up and why I'd left the cheerleading squad. And because the most popular rumor was that Kira had been dating Christian until I'd "stolen" him away, it had been really hard to defend myself. Not without exposing the Smitten Kittens as SOS.

So I kept my mouth shut. I denied what I could, hoping the rest would eventually fade away. It was amazing how differently people treated me now that I wasn't their spirit savior. I was…ordinary.

"Hey, Tessa," Chris Townsend said as I walked into language arts. The sound of his deep voice startled me. Gosh, I was really on edge!

"Oh, hi." I glanced around the classroom, the circular arrangement of the desks, the stacks of books that overflowed from the shelves, feeling a little lost.

"You okay?" Chris asked, tilting his head toward mine.

"Uh-huh." But I wasn't. I was decidedly not okay. Chris was nice enough; I didn't want to worry him. He was on the football team—a meaty linebacker with a great chance at a scholarship. He had light blond hair and a perfect speckling of freckles across the bridge of his nose. And lucky for him, he looked fantastic in uniform. Kira had pointed it out on a number of occasions. The ladies of Washington High were crazy about him. Maybe I would have been too, if I didn't have Aiden.

Chris smiled at me. "Well, I'm here for you if you wanna talk," he said, backing away, his sneakers squeaking on the linoleum floor.

I nodded, not sure if he was trying to be comforting or trying to ask me out. Seemed that since I'd become single, there were a lot of guys trying to "comfort" me. But they didn't understand that Aiden and I were still figuring out our relationship.

"Take your seats," Ms. Lipton said as she stomped into the room wearing her leather combat boots. She had short, spiky black hair and a closet full of flannels. She was pretty but in desperate need of some lipstick. Still, I enjoyed her class.

I sat down at the wood-top desk and folded my hands in front of me, thinking over what Leona had said the day before. Was I home when someone broke in, asleep in my bed while an intruder tiptoed around my house? I shivered.

"Ms. Crimson?" Ms. Lipton asked. I glanced up quickly only to meet her very stern expression.

"Yes?"

"You were mumbling," she said, squinting her dark eyes. "We have a test—are you unprepared?"

I gasped. Of course I was prepared. What a silly question. "I studied," I answered, trying to flash a winning smile. But by the expression on her face, I could tell I was unconvincing.

After another second of scrutiny, she nodded and hopped off her desk to grab a stack of papers that was sitting on its wood surface. She counted out the tests row by row, and we passed them backward as usual. When Ralph Moss turned around to give me my test, he grinned. "How's it going, Sex Kitten?" he asked.

Gross. I'd caught his dimpled rear…well, I'd *seen* his dimpled rear through the back windshield of his Bronco two years ago. He was cheating on his girlfriend with a foreign exchange student from Brazil. But I was pretty sure the only reason Magdalena was in that truck was because she didn't speak English. Ralph was a tool of epic proportions.

"I'm not on the squad anymore, Ralph," I said as politely as possible. No need to feed into his negativity. "And besides, it's *Smitten.*"

"Not what I heard," he said with a laugh before turning around.

Sigh. That joke had gotten old. No one ever actually came out and accused me of anything scandalous—my sources were secondhand (aka: Kira).

As I turned to pass the test behind me to Megan Wright, she smiled. "Don't listen to Ralph. He's an idiot." She flipped her blonde hair over her shoulder and rolled her eyes in his direction. "Remember when he cheated on Jessica with Maggie Jimenez?"

"I think so." Of course I remembered. I'd seen Maggie's entire anatomy and physiology and captured it on film. Good gravy! It'd just occurred to me that the copy-Kitten had highly sensitive information. There was more at stake than just our reputations.

Megan nodded. "It was totally weird. You know the only reason he was able to hook up with Maggie was because she didn't understand English. If she did, she would have known that he was a complete butthead." I laughed. My thoughts exactly.

"Ladies, do you mind?" Ms. Lipton asked, tapping her black boot on the shiny classroom floor.

"Sorry," I answered, turning back around. I didn't like being scolded.

"By the way," Megan whispered from behind me. "The cheer squad's not nearly as good now that you're gone. Caught their practice the other day, and their cheers were pretty lame. You really rocked as captain. Way more original."

I pressed my lips into a smile and glanced down at the sheet on my desk. It was sweet of her to say, but my stomach dropped. I missed the squad, being a part of something. Dismissing the thought, I looked closer at my test. I apparently had other problems to think about because none of the questions on my test looked even remotely familiar. I rubbed my eyes and checked it again. Nope. Not a clue.

My cell phone vibrated in my pocket. For a second, my heart sped up, but then I remembered that it wasn't the SOS phone—it was just mine. I hadn't gotten used to that yet. With a cautionary glance toward Ms. Lipton, I slid my pink cell out of my pocket and looked at the incoming number. I didn't recognize the area code.

I clicked the phone off and slipped it back into my jeans, turning back to my test. Honestly, had I even read *Death of a Salesman*? It sounded tragic.

"Ms. Crimson?"

I looked up, startled by Ms. Lipton's voice. She was sitting at her desk, staring at me. Next to her was a freshman I barely recognized, clutching a slip of white paper. He handed it to her and walked out.

"It's from Principal Pelli," my teacher said. "He wants to see you." She pursed her lips as if the next part disgusted her in unspeakable ways. "You can come in during lunch to finish the test."

"Really?" That was excellent news! I'd be studying all through the morning. Hm, where could I get CliffsNotes at this time of day?

"Meow," Ralph Moss said as I stood up.

"Moss, I'm beating your ass after school," Chris Townsend called from across the room. I smiled a little. It was nice of him to stick up for me.

"Enough, gentlemen." Ms. Lipton shook her head.

I shoved my pen into the front pocket of my backpack and grabbed my test, handing it off to Ms. Lipton.

She took it, her face tightening at the sight of my blank page. Ms. Lipton rolled her eyes and handed me the hall pass. "See you at lunch, Ms. Crimson."

I made my way out the classroom door and into the deserted hallway. I was a little creeped out. The corridor was empty, but I couldn't shake that paranoid feeling. That feeling of being watched. Having someone break into your house will do that to a person.

I wrapped my arms around myself and began the long walk to the principal's office, listening to the echo of my footsteps.

"Hey, prez."

I twirled around to see Chloe Ferril hang her dark leather jacket in her locker. Immediately I was reminded of my vow to investigate her. The corner of my mouth twitched.

"Chloe." I nodded in her direction.

Since last year, her style had gone from vixen to vampire. She dressed in goth clothes, even going so far as to paint her ragged fingernails bloodred. But I couldn't complain. At least her breasts were covered up now.

She smirked. "How's Aiden?"

I nearly hissed. "He's great. Thanks for asking." She knew

it got under my skin when she inquired about my ex. That was probably why she did it every time she saw me. Which, thankfully, wasn't very often.

Chloe laughed, tilting her head so that her smooth blonde hair flowed over one shoulder. "I'm glad to hear that. Tell him I said science isn't the same without him, okay?"

"Sure." I most certainly would *not*.

She smiled and slammed her locker shut before traipsing off in the opposite direction, her boots thudding on the hall floor.

"I'll get right on that," I mumbled as she walked away. Well, she definitely shot up on my suspect list. I made a mental note of her locker number and decided that I'd pick the lock after school and see if she was hiding anything inside there. Then maybe tonight I would take a drive by her house.

I pulled my lips into a pout. Seeing Chloe today was particularly irksome. At least I didn't have to deal with Christian. The brother-sister duo would have been a little too much, especially right now.

My phone vibrated in my pocket again. I exhaled, slightly unnerved by Chloe's mention of Aiden, and slid out my cell to check the number. It was the same unfamiliar one from before.

"Hello?" I asked, my eyebrows pulled together.

"Tessa? Hey, it's Mary."

I squealed. "Mary! How are you?" Mary Rudick was our ex-captain and the founder of SOS. She was, like, the ultimate in pep preservation, so she'd called at the perfect moment. "I haven't talked to you in forever!" We barely spoke now that she was going to school in California.

"I know," she apologized, her voice raspy but upbeat as always. "I've been going crazy with these courses. College. Is. Super-hard."

"That's what Aiden tells me."

"Aiden? He—I mean, I thought Kira told me you two broke up."

"Sort of," I said, my stomach turning at the mention of it. "But we're…um, anyway, he goes to Washington State now. He's always studying."

"Oh, well, that's good," she said, then paused. "I've been there a few times. It's a beautiful campus."

I frowned. "I've never been up there." At that, I wondered why none of my sessions with Aiden had taken place on campus. Hm. I'd have to ask him if I could come visit.

"Actually," Mary said, sounding suddenly serious. "I was wondering if you had a sec. I wanted to talk with you about something."

Even though I loved to talk cheer, there was the pesky matter of the note in my hand from Principal Pelli's office. "Do you think I could call you when I get to lunch?" I asked, reaching behind me to rub at my back muscle. "I'm at school, and Principal Pelli just summoned me to the office."

"Are you in trouble?" Mary asked.

"Don't think so. Probably just a new student to shadow me or something." I swallowed hard, remembering the last time a new student came to this school. He ended up with his tongue in my mouth. Gross. "But I'd love to catch up," I added into the phone, shaking the uncomfortable memory.

"For sure," Mary said. "It's…no big deal. I just wanted to touch base. I've missed you girls and I couldn't get through on the SOS phone, so I thought I'd try your cell."

My heart skipped a beat. None of us had told Mary that we'd dissolved SOS. When she went to school here, she'd put her all into SOS. In fact, nearly every detail of the society came from her. She might freak if she found out we stopped without consulting her, and, well, we didn't want to disappoint her.

"Sounds great," I said, gnawing at the corner of my bottom lip. "The squad will be stoked to talk to you." And they would. I'd just have to make sure they kept it short and sweet. I wouldn't want Mary's college workload to be impaired by stress. And I certainly didn't want her getting wind of this copy-Kitten nonsense. After all, her rep was on the line too.

"Talk soon," she sang.

I took a deep breath and shoved my phone back into my pocket. This was a very delicate situation, one I'd have to take charge of. Whatever we did, we'd have to act fast. And most importantly, we'd need to keep it quiet.

When I entered the front office, the smell of paper and potpourri immediately struck me. The dark-haired, middle-aged secretary behind the desk waved. She was great like that. Total spirit addict.

"Morning, Tessa. How are you?" Her desk tag said Mrs. Lambert, but she let all of the students call her Peggy. Unfortunately a few people called her Piggy behind her back, but I always made sure to correct them. There was no excuse for unwarranted rude behavior.

"I'm doing very well," I said, smiling. "Thanks for asking. Principal Pelli sent for me?" I handed her the note and reached up to adjust the ribbon of my ponytail, stopping when I realized that the ribbon wasn't there. I instead smoothed out my hair in one nervous movement.

"Oh, right." Peggy snapped her fingers. "He wanted to talk to you about homecoming."

"Homecoming?" Perspiration was beginning to gather under my arms, which was a disturbing development. I'd never had perspiration problems before. "Why me?"

"Because you're head of the Washington High welcoming committee. If it's a problem, I'm sure he can call Kira—"

"No," I interrupted. "I'm still the president of the homecoming committee. He's right. Sorry." I didn't want to burden Kira with anything more and hey, at least I was still in charge of something. "He's expecting me?" I asked.

Peggy reached up to put the end of her pen between her teeth. "Yeah, you can go in." She nodded toward his door.

"Thanks," I tried to sound perky. I walked across the carpet, and just before I opened his glass door, Peggy called out to me.

"Tessa?"

"Yes?"

"The squad's not quite the same without you." She looked nostalgic. I remembered her at the games last year, front row, painted face. My cheeks warmed as I met her small eyes.

"Thanks," I murmured, dropping my head as I turned to walk into the principal's office.

SOS
NEW POLICIES

Dear Clients,

As a matter of safety, SOS has decided to take our investigations public. In the past, our services have always been confidential, but we do not feel that exposing infidelity privately has been an effective deterrent to cheaters.

For the protection of all girls, the Naughty List will now be released to the public. It will be posted on our new blog at www.thecheaterreports.blogspot.com. There will also be updates, pictures, and videos available for viewing.

Although our identities are still confidential, our services are not. So spread the word. SOS is stomping out heartbreaking countywide.

And remember, cheaters never win. Especially with SOS on the case!

Keep kicking ass,
SOS ☺

SOS www.thecheaterreport.blogspot.com
Text: 555-1863
Exposing Cheaters for Over Three Years

CHAPTER SIX

"HAVE A SEAT, TESSA." PRINCIPAL PELLI MOTIONED to the boxy wooden chair in front of his desk. I'd been a little nervous before, but now, actually being in his office made me very uneasy. The return of SOS had frayed my nerves.

"What's going on?" I asked, sounding guilty even though I was sure I'd done nothing wrong. At least, nothing lately.

"It's about the squad." The principal took off his glasses and began cleaning them with the white handkerchief from his desk. "We have a problem."

Lucy in the sky with diamonds! Did he know about the copy-Kitten? Did he know what we'd been doing for the past two years? "Problem?" I squeaked.

Principal Pelli nodded, slipping his glasses back on his nose. "I've sat in on a few of the Smitten Kittens' practices, Tessa. Things are not looking good. Coach Taylor is concerned."

"He shouldn't be. Kira is completely capable and—"

"I know she's your friend." Principal Pelli held up his hand to stop me. "But last routine, they had to call an ambulance after Izzie fell during a lift."

"Human pyramid," I corrected.

He raised his eyebrows.

"Sorry. You were saying?" I wasn't sure what exactly Principal Pelli wanted from me. I wasn't the captain.

"Listen, Tessa," he said in a quiet voice. "The squad has been very popular over the last few years, bringing in tons of revenue from the games. Lord knows the team wasn't attracting the crowds," he mumbled.

The Wildcats had been on a three-year losing streak until they'd made Aiden point guard for his senior year. I smiled. He was so athletically gifted.

"But after last season's playoff debacle," Principal Pelli continued, "things haven't been the same. The Smitten Kittens don't inspire the image we want for the school, and they definitely aren't preselling many tickets. Part of that is due to your hasty exit, and part is due to Kira's inexperience. If I don't see some changes quickly, I'm going to have to ask her to step down." He paused before delivering the final blow. "I need your help."

My face grew hot as embarrassment washed over me. It was one thing for my personal trainer and hairdresser to know about my meltdown in center court last year, but it was something completely different for the principal—the education chief of staff—to call what happened a debacle. I mean, he was right. But it still stung.

"How can I help?" I asked quietly.

"I want you back on the squad. I want you to make sure that the homecoming game goes off without a hitch. Or an ambulance. It's our biggest game of the season."

I shook my head, confused. "But sir, I'm not on the squad anymore. I can't just... show up in uniform."

"Can't you?"

I looked down into my lap, perplexed by this new turn of events. I'd given the power to Kira. It wouldn't be right for me to just take it away without letting her have a real shot. Besides, it wasn't totally my decision. Smitten Kitten rules would require a vote. "No," I said, meeting his gaze. "I can't."

He exhaled loudly. "Then I'm sorry, but I—"

"However," I interrupted, holding up my index finger. "I *will* sit in on the practices and help the squad put together some cheers for the game."

He smiled, looking relieved. "Thank you, Tessa."

I nodded and stood up. My anxiety returned as I began to consider how I would tell Kira about this conversation, but then I decided that maybe it was best if I didn't. Kira wasn't great with pressure. And it would be totally natural for me to show up more, given the recent turn of events.

Yeah, Kira and stress didn't mix. Last time we went to our annual cheer competition, she'd puked in her megaphone during the finals. It was horrific.

After closing the principal's door behind me, I passed through the front office. Peggy was giving me a wayward glance—like maybe she'd been listening over the intercom the entire time. I tried to look cheerful, but the pain in my back made me pause mid-step.

"Everything okay?" Peggy asked. I winced but forced a smile.

"Peachy." Truth was, I felt sourer than I wanted to admit.

When lunch arrived, I found out that the Smitten Kittens were having a squad meeting (that I wasn't invited to), and I was left to hurry through my test, then plop down in the cafeteria among the smells of processed meat and steamed corn. It wasn't a really great day, and now I only had a few minutes to regroup.

"Hey, Tessa," Chris Townsend said, coming to stand at the end of the lunch table.

I turned in my seat, surprised to feel more than a little relieved. Sitting by yourself was rather humiliating, especially when the word around campus was that I was a desperate ex-Kitten who still hooked up with her ex-boyfriend (sort of).

"Hi," I replied, motioning for Chris to sit down. He offered me a flawless smile as he eased onto the seat. His cologne was a bit stronger than I preferred, but his adorable button-up shirt made up for that. I was trying really hard to notice the little things about people. The barista at Starbucks said it'd be good for me.

"So I was wondering," he said quietly. "Would you come to my party Saturday after next? If not, it's totally cool. I just—"

"Oh…" I hadn't been expecting that. It wasn't like I had plans, but—

"Party?" Izzie squealed, appearing suddenly and plopping down in the seat next to Chris. She looked positively elated. I knew I'd been out of the loop for while, but it seemed odd for her to be that pleased. Izzie didn't really like jocks. "Is it a costume party?" She beamed. "I love those."

"No…" he said slowly.

"Tessa will be there," Leona said, walking over to sit across from us. Her lips were dark red, making her resemble a fifties pinup model. It was a fabulous look for her! I hoped this meant she'd worked things out with Marco.

"I will?" I darted a glance around the table just as Leona kicked my shoe.

"Yes," she said through gritted teeth. "We'll all be there."

"Awesome." Chris grinned, looking completely stoked that it'd been decided. I felt a little uneasy but forced back a tight smile. I liked to leave my weekends open in case Aiden came to town.

"Sounds great."

I waited until he was gone and crossing the crowded lunchroom before turning to face Leona. "What was that about?"

Leona popped a stick of gum in her mouth, looking bored. "You'll see," she said with a wink.

Izzie giggled from next to me. They were definitely up to something, but it would have to wait. My phone vibrated in my pocket.

Holy Macintosh! It was Mary again. Before I could decide what to do, the ringing stopped. Had she hung up? Hm. Maybe she'd misdialed. I decided to wait to see if she'd call back. It could have been considered stalling, since I had no idea what I'd tell her about SOS or cheerleading, but I liked to think of it as proper etiquette. Oprah once pointed out that a person should plan what they're going to say before speaking up. And Oprah was never wrong.

After lunch, Izzie and Leona went to the library for study hall as I slowly made my way to sociology class. I was halfway to my locker when I heard it—a new rumor. I only caught pieces of the story as I walked, but it still made me stop cold in my tracks.

SOS.

It was Robert Bullard. SOS (the real one) had caught him last year, cheating on his girlfriend with her cousin. It had been a really messy assignment. Lots of stakeouts, lots of...positions. Gross. Sometimes I hated thinking about those days.

I glided over to the right side of the hall and bent down, pretending to take a drink from the water fountain as I listened.

"Yeah," he said, his nasally voice tinged with anger. "Apparently some bitches put together a website about cheating boyfriends."

I choked on the water.

"No way." Robert's friend Shane rubbed at his pimply chin. "Wait. That would totally explain that break-in!"

"Yep." Robert shook his head. "Heard about that. Some dude's computer got fucked. Then there was this list of guys posted on the internet. Something called the 'Naughty List.'" He scoffed.

"And no one knows who's behind it?"

I gulped, my breath coming out in gasps. The copy-Kitten must have done something. A…website? I was about to hyperventilate.

"Nope," Robert said. I sighed with relief. "But they call themselves SOS."

"Oh, shit, man!" Shane said. "Do you think that's how Melinda found out about you last year?"

"Probably," Robert said, looking angry. As if SOS was the problem and not his cheating. "Like you said, it explains a lot. All I know is whoever it is, they're going down."

"I'm with you, bro." Shane reached out to slap hands with him.

I straightened, my heart in my throat, and backed away from the fountain. Just as I was about to hurry down the hall, Robert called out to me.

"Hey, Tessa," he said, his voice making goose bumps crawl across my flesh. (Once you'd heard someone talk dirty, even the most innocent remarks felt tainted.)

"Hi," I replied, forcing a smile.

Robert grinned as Shane ogled me. "Heard about you and Aiden," he said. "That's too bad; he's a real good guy."

I couldn't tell if he was being honest or checking to see if he had the go-ahead to ask me out. By the pervy smirk on his lips, I decided it was the latter.

"Thanks. I'll tell him you said so."

His smile faltered. "Cool," he answered, nodding. "Well, see you around."

My heart was still racing. They'd just been talking about SOS. They *knew* there was an SOS. And now it was just a matter of time until they found out the Smitten Kittens had started it! My fingers began to tremble, and I started to walk down the hall.

"By the way," Robert called after me. "The squad sucks now. You were the best one."

"And the hottest," Shane added, and they both chuckled.

I swallowed hard and raised my hand in a gesture of acknowledgment, blinking back my tears. SOS was out. Now all of our tails were on the chopping block.

I wasn't feeling emotionally stable enough to endure Mr. Rothstein's latest sociology rant—probably a lesson on ethics again or the cruelty of popularity in today's society. Instead of heading to class, I took out my phone and dialed Aiden's dorm room.

"Please answer," I murmured, feeling the flood of tears that was about to break through me.

"Hey, it's Aiden. I'm not here, so leave a message."

My heart nearly crumbled. I needed him. Right now. "Aiden, it's me," I said into the phone, my voice cracking. "When you get this, can you call me back? It's an emergency." He wasn't answering. Seemed like lately, he was never there when I needed him.

"Hey, Tess."

I jumped and spun around, clutching my phone like a weapon. "Joel!"

He laughed, holding up his hands as he stepped back. "Um... have you been taking a lot of self-defense classes lately? Because you're starting to scare me. You're like Master Tessa with the kung fu phone."

I smiled, breathing deeply to calm myself down. At least my back spasm had temporarily disappeared. "More grasshopper than master."

"Naw. You're a total black belt." Joel checked his watch and glanced back at me. "You're late," he said. "Were you calling for a ride or something?"

I knitted my eyebrows. "Ride? Oh, no. I was desperately trying to get a hold of Aiden." Suddenly the worry came back over me. SOS. People knew.

"Kira told me you and Aiden broke up," Joel said.

"Sort of." I really wished people would stop pointing that out. I mean, did I go around making verbal observations about anyone else's love life? Or "sort of" love life?

"Sounds complicated," Joel said, making a face. "And I think complicated"—he leaned toward me—"kinda bites."

I nodded. "Believe me, it does."

We both sighed at the same time and looked at each other. "Jinx?" he asked.

"No, I think we have to say the same thing for it to be a jinx. Sighs don't count—"

"Don't count—" He broke in to finish my sentence.

We both paused. "Jinx." We laughed.

"Okay," he said. "Don't talk yet. What were you desperately

in need of? Now, I'm no Aiden Wilder—mostly because I suck at sports—but maybe I can be of service in another way. I'm a good listener...."

My smile faded. I needed Aiden. I had major life drama to deal with. First, Principal Pelli's ultimatum with the squad and then the SOS outing—which would most certainly lead to a Smitten Kittens outing, eventually ending in social upheaval. It was almost too much. I wanted to talk to someone, but I didn't think Kira's boyfriend was the obvious choice.

"Sorry, Joel," I said. "It's a secret."

He smiled deviously, and his offset tooth looked extra-adorable under his curved lip. "Secret, huh?" he whispered, leaning closer to me. "You know that only makes me want to know more, right?"

Hm. He had a good point. "It's not important," I said, in an attempt to dismiss it. But when he rubbed his palms together excitedly, I knew I'd said too much.

"Okay." I took his arm to pull him closer. "But you can't say anything. Not a word."

"Um..." He looked around the hallway, swinging his head back and forth dramatically. "Cross my heart and hope to die, stick a needle in my eye." He paused, crinkling his nose. "Not really. Not the needle thing—it sounds much too painful."

I stared at him for a second, then laughed. Even though Joel and I hadn't known each other that long, I liked him. He seemed completely trustworthy. And right now, I couldn't say that about a lot of people.

"So Principal Pelli called me into his office," I whispered.

"Troublemaker," Joel teased.

I gave him a mock glare before continuing. "He..." I swallowed hard. "He wants me to take back the captainship of the Smitten Kittens."

Joel straightened up and ran his hand through his brown hair. "Whoa. That's bad."

"I know. Kira would die. I have no idea how to tell—"

"Hey!" Kira called, jogging down the hall, her cheer skirt flopping up as she came to stand next to Joel. She hooked her arm in his. "I've been looking everywhere for you," she said to him, smiling.

"Right. Sorry." Joel stared at the ground, looking worried. I regretted telling him anything, because it would surely put him in an awkward position. He looked at me. "I was...helping Tessa with something."

Kira glanced between me and Joel. She furrowed her brow. "With what?"

"K, I need to talk to you," I said firmly. I didn't want Joel to be the one to tell her first. Once Kira heard that the principal and coach didn't believe in her cheerleading ability, her self-esteem would be blown. But I had to say something. Right? I mean, how else would it look if I started coming to all the practices and telling her what to do?

Joel cleared his throat and shook his head slightly. "I have to go," he said loudly. "But Tessa, I'll get in touch with you later about that *physics* assignment."

"Ugh," Kira said. "I hate fortune-tellers."

Both Joel and I turned to her and then back to each other. He smiled. "Don't start on it without me, okay?" he asked.

Obviously he didn't want me to tell Kira about the squad stuff, and maybe he was right. I was ready to take any excuse to get out of what would be an uncomfortable conversation with Kira. And besides, I had bigger pom-poms to shake.

"Okay," I agreed.

Joel mimed wiping sweat from his forehead and then leaned down to give Kira a quick kiss on the nose. "I'll catch up with you after school," he said, untangling his arm from hers.

"But I thought…" Kira looked confused, a pout pulling at her well-glossed lips. "Never mind. I'll see you then."

Joel gave her hand a quick squeeze before walking away and down the hall. When I looked back at Kira, she was crying.

I widened my eyes and reached out to touch her arm. "Weeping willow, K! What's wrong?"

"I think he's breaking up with me," she sobbed. "You know what I realized, Tess? He said space, as in *needing* space! He doesn't like me anymore."

"My word, no!" I immediately wrapped my arm around her in a hug, her blonde curls tickling my face. I couldn't believe she was thinking so negatively. "Hey," I said, pressing my lips into a smile as I pulled back to look her in the eyes. "He's totally smitten with you, K. He practically told me so earlier."

"Earlier?" she squeaked, blinking quickly. She dabbed at her black mascara, which had begun to pool under her eyes. "What did he say?"

I rotated my torso a few times as I spoke, stretching out my back. "I saw him in the hall after the meeting and mentioned the space thing. Sorry, K. It just slipped out. Anyway, he said that he thought maybe you wanted a break, but I assured him that you didn't. And he was completely relieved." I smiled, but Kira didn't look happy.

"You guys were talking about our relationship?"

"Not really, we just…" I exhaled. I'd really thought it would cheer her up, knowing that he still adored her. But now she was getting upset instead. "Look, he loves you, K. That was all he said."

Her jaw clenched just a little before she finally smiled. Kira had been stressed lately, and I didn't need to make it worse by bringing up her boyfriend or mentioning cheerleading. No, I would have to go about this differently. Carefully.

Just as I was about to apologize again, Leona came running down the hall with Izzie in tow. "Bathroom," she called. "Now!"

My stomach twisted at the urgency in her voice. Kira and I darted ahead of them into the girls' room, exchanging a nervous glance.

Then the bathroom door swung open, banging against the wall with a loud clang. Leona was standing there with her cell phone in hand, her brown hair wild around her face.

"Holy crap, where have you two been?" she demanded, letting go of Izzie's sleeve.

"I was looking for Joel," Kira said, splashing cold water on her face. "And Tessa…was talking to him. To Joel, I mean." She paused, water dripping down her cheeks before she reached over to crank out a paper towel.

"Look," I said toward the girls, making my tone very serious. "Before you say anything, I need to tell you . . . I heard something awful in the hallway."

Leona narrowed her eyes and looked me over. "What kind of awful? Spill."

I took a deep breath. "I overheard Robert Bullard talking about SOS. He knew the name." My heart was pounding in my chest, but Leona didn't look nearly as stunned as I'd thought she should. "Did you hear me?" I asked.

"Tell her," Izzie said, nudging Leona with her elbow. My breath caught in my chest. The floral smell in the bathroom mixed with my newly perspiring underarms was making me nauseous.

"Don't get your bloomers in a bunch," Leona warned. "But you have to look at this." She held out her cell, and I leaned over its tiny display. I squinted. It showed a new message from the SOS e-mail account.

"They have a blog?" Well, it wasn't a website, but close enough. And just as bad.

Kira pushed in next to me. "Really? That's awesome. Why didn't we think of that?"

"Because we were top secret, stupid," Leona snapped.

"Or maybe you didn't know how to set up a blog," Kira shot back.

Leona scoffed, brushing her bangs away from her face. "Please, blogs are so easy to set up, even you could do it. And we both know how hopeless you are with technology. Hello, Facebook disaster of sophomore year."

"I've been working on it!" Kira shouted back.

My brain was going fuzzy with tension overload when the bathroom door swung open, nailing Leona on the shoulder.

"What the hell?" she screamed. The culprit behind the swinging door was Chloe Ferril.

Chloe's red mouth spread into a sarcastic grin as she looked from face to face. "Did they relocate cheer practice to the bathroom now?" She laughed to herself and waltzed in, her boots echoing through the tiled room. "Probably a good idea, since your routines are shit."

Kira growled under her breath as Chloe elbowed past us into the handicapped stall and closed the door. Leona came to stand next to me, rubbing her shoulder. "Are you setting up the surveillance?" she whispered in my ear, nodding toward the closed metal door. "I just know it's her. Bitch hit me with a door."

"And my routines rock," Kira hissed quietly, biting at her nail and sidling up next to me. "We just need more practice. God, I hate her. You should totally fight her again, Tess. Only this time, kick *her* ass."

I darted a glance at her. I felt a hand on my shoulder as Izzie joined us. "I can't believe she's using the handicap stall," she whispered. "That's so tacky. She's not even disabled."

The toilet flushed with a loud *whoosh*, and we scattered to our respective sinks, as though we hadn't been loitering.

"Ready for homecoming?" Chloe asked, stepping up behind Kira and me to run her hands under the water.

"I'm not a cheerleader, remember?" I answered, holding her stare.

She turned off the faucet before shaking out her hands into the sink. "That's right." She winked. "Forgot."

She moved back, studying her reflection as she brushed her hands through her long blonde hair—the only evidence of the old Chloe, the schemer who'd tried to steal Aiden. She sighed. "Well, good luck with that," she said, shooting a glance at Kira.

"Thanks, wench," Kira returned, turning away from her.

I half expected Leona to trip Chloe as she walked out, but instead she held open the door for her. Once Chloe was gone, Leona pushed the door closed and turned back to us, her mouth hanging open.

"Did you see that?" she asked.

"Yeah," Kira said, bending toward the mirror to reapply her lip gloss. "Black is so not her color."

"Not that," Leona said. "She didn't even use soap to wash her hands! That's completely unsanitary."

"And totally nasty," Izzie echoed.

Although I fully agreed that hygiene was important, we needed to focus. I'd been hoping that Robert had been mistaken about SOS breaking into someone's house to wipe their computer files. I mean, SOS had hacked plenty of computers, but to clear the hard drive? That was harsh. Still it was obvious after the latest message—and now the news of the blog—that this faux Kitten meant business.

I rested my shaking hands on the cold porcelain of the sink. I'd never thought the copy-Kitten's ruse would get this far. *Saying* you're the Society of Smitten Kittens was one thing, but actually *performing missions?* That was appalling!

"I meant to tell you," Izzie said, looking at me wide-eyed. "While Sam and I were arguing last night, my grandpa clicked in to tell me that someone had broken into his garage. He didn't think anything was stolen, but my bet is that some of our equipment is gone."

"Figured that," Leona said. "I don't blame them. I had an impressive spy gear collection." She looked at Izzie. "And sorry about the arguing with Sam."

Izzie waved it off with her hand. "It was nothing. No bigs."

I wanted to crawl into a pint of Ben and Jerry's ice cream. This copy-Kitten had rep-assassinated us *and* stolen our goods. Would the horror never end?

I let the voices of the squad fade to background noise

for a minute as I concentrated hard. I rubbed my eyes and, when I finally opened them, I stared at my reflection. Blotchy. Scared.

"I have to go," I said suddenly, spinning to face them. I had an assignment to complete.

"Now?" Leona asked. "You look like you're going to puke, Tess. Maybe you should sit down."

"Ew, on the toilet?" Kira asked, scrunching her nose in the direction of the stall.

"Maybe we can go to the mall?" Izzie interjected, obviously still itching to use her plastic.

Leona and Kira seemed to consider this, but I interrupted. "No," I said. "You girls need to practice, get your cheers in order. I have other business to handle. Business involving a certain pouty blonde with an affection for the unholy."

"Black is still not her color," Kira added.

"Totally," I agreed, keeping my voice authoritative. (It helped inspire confidence.) "Now, I'll run my surveillance and call to set up a rendezvous point for later. Agreed?"

The Kittens stared back at me, looking a bit stunned.

"Whoa," Leona said, a smile tugging at the corners of her dark lips. "You sounded like the old Tessa just now."

"It was pretty cool." Izzie giggled.

"Well…good." I straightened my posture. The old Tessa would have totally kicked spying tush right about now.

The bell overhead rang and Kira groaned. "I've got to jet. Practice immediately after school," she said, holding up her finger in warning to the girls. "Spread the word."

"Yes, captain," Leona said with an eye roll and a salute.

Kira glanced at me. "Good luck, Tess." She smiled supportively and I nodded, watching as she left.

.   After Leona and Izzie followed her, I waited and turned to examine my reflection once again. Did I still know how to spy? Investigating someone like Chloe, someone I was clearly connected with, was a conflict of interest. Would I be able to objectively collect information?

The skin under my eyes looked puffy, and I sighed heavily. Then with only the sound of my shoes echoing on the tile floor, I walked up to the bathroom door, yanked it open, and headed out.

It was time to get back to basics. It was time to channel the skirt.

ASSIGNMENTS 1 & 2

5:00 P.M., SEPTEMBER 15

Riley and Jenn were sitting together in a vinyl booth at Mel's Pizza sharing a slice as the operative observed them. Both seemed a little distracted, but every so often, Riley leaned in to give Jenn a quick kiss. The operative squinted, trying to understand.

Both Riley and Jenn were starting relationships with other people—or so it seemed. How could they so boldly flaunt their infidelity, then act affectionate in public, as though nothing were wrong?

The operative adjusted her black baseball cap downward before reaching for the straw of her cherry Coke, all the while peering from beneath the cap's bill. She'd never seen a case like this. It would require a serious cheater case study.

Just then, the door to the pizza shop jangled open. The operative glanced over and nearly choked on her carbonated beverage. It was Megan Wright...and she looked stunned.

Riley had been resting his head on Jenn's shoulder, laughing easily when Megan walked in. Living life, unaware that his sins were about to confront him. When he saw her, he immediately straightened up, but the hurt on Megan's face was plain. Even as she bravely tried to smile.

"Meg!" Jenn called out, waving her over. "Sit with us."

The operative tilted her head, enjoying this turn of events. There'd be no way Megan could act her way through this. She was about to get busted. The operative slipped her hand into the pocket of her shorts and pulled out a tiny metal device, which she slipped in her ear. From across the room, she'd be able to hear anything. Even a whisper. Thank you, infomercial.

Megan looked from Jenn to Riley, then she pursed her lips and nodded. She walked over to the booth and slid in across from Jenn—directly next to Riley. The tension was delicious. The operative happily picked up her slice of pizza and took a bite.

"I haven't seen you in forever," Jenn said to Megan, reaching in her purse to pull out a tube of lip gloss. "Where've you been?"

"Um…I've been studying. My classes are tough this semester." Megan glanced sideways at Riley, but he kept his eyes trained on the table.

"You're such a nerd." Jenn laughed, touching her mouth with the napkin.

Riley started to open his mouth, then looked quickly back down at the table. Had he been about to defend his accomplice? The operative smiled. Riley exposing himself like that would be a lethal mistake.

Jenn sighed and glanced at her watch. "I have to babysit in half an hour," she said to Riley. "You ready?"

He nodded, his face turning a deep pink. Jenn looked at him strangely, then rolled her eyes and slid from the booth. "I'll be right back; I have to pee first." She took one last sip from her drink before heading past the counter to the back restrooms.

"I'm so sorry, Meg," Riley murmured to Megan the minute his girlfriend was out of sight. "I didn't mean to—"

"I have to go," Megan said, the vinyl of the seat sticking to her thighs as she moved away from him. "I can't do this anymore. Tell Jenn I'll call her later." Megan grabbed her purse angrily before jumping to her feet.

The operative tilted her head. For a second, she admired Megan's loyalty to her friend. But what she saw next made her lip curl. Megan paused at the end of the booth; suddenly she leaned down, her blonde hair falling forward to block the operative's view. She bent toward Riley's ear.

"I love you too," she whispered. Then, without even buying what she came for, she walked out of the shop.

The operative's stomach turned. She was momentarily stunned by Megan's careless statement. Megan wasn't allowed to tell him that. She wasn't allowed to do that! This was treachery in the first degree.

Reaching up to remove the listening device from her ear, the operative accidentally bumped into the table, knocking over her cherry Coke.

"Shit," she said, jumping away as the liquid streamed to the floor. When Riley glanced over his shoulder at her, she nearly passed out. But he chuckled at the party foul without seeming to register the operative's presence.

Exhaling in relief, she then grabbed her leather backpack and headed toward the exit, trying to wrap her mind around the interactions she'd been witnessing. This was too complicated, and she wasn't sure she'd be able to prove anything.

"I know, Tate."

The operative stopped mid-step and glanced down the hallway to the bathroom. Jenn was standing there, pressing her cell to one ear.

"I'll be there," she murmured. "Ten thirty tomorrow at Skinner Butte." She smiled. "I'll see you then."

Before Jenn could look up, the operative turned on her heels and made for the front door. Score one for the spy.

CHAPTER SEVEN

I YANKED MY T-SHIRT OVER MY HEAD AS THE midday sun filtered in through my sheer bedroom curtains. My parents were out of town until tonight doing a gig at a coffeehouse in Vancouver, which was a good thing. I was pretty sure they'd be unhappy with me cutting school. But it was a gorgeous day, and I had a mission—I was already feeling like the old me.

I went right for it. The skirt was tucked under my winter sweaters, where I liked to keep it hidden. Sometimes when I was feeling down, I'd wear the uniform for moral support. But I never told anyone that. It was sort of sad. But—this was different.

I wiggled out of my dark denim jeans and tossed them into the corner. Then I smoothed my hands reverently over the polyester fabric of the skirt. One foot at time, I stepped into it, pulling the waistband slowly over my hips and thighs until it rested at my waist.

Next I shook out the sleeveless top before pulling it down over my flesh-colored bra. Wow. I must have been downing more Frappuccinos than I realized—my cleavage was overflowing—okay for in the house, but not really game appropriate. Sort of like how Chloe used to dress. Provocatively.

I slid my feet into my official regulation-style sneakers, tying the laces tightly. Without missing a beat, I crossed over to my vanity, adrenaline already pumping. This felt right. This felt natural. I knew I'd be able to think and plan more clearly with the power of the skirt.

I picked up a ponytail holder and gathered my hair in one hand, securing the elastic with the other. Once I had it fastened, I selected a maroon ribbon from the bunch I kept draped across the top of my dresser. Holding it delicately, I wrapped it around my ponytail and tied it into a perfect bow. I took a step back, looked myself over, and smiled. My ritual was complete.

In uniform—albeit a tight one—I was in control. My cheer skirt (a little short), my top (a little revealing), and even my ribbon (perky as ever!) were what I was born to wear.

Suddenly I wasn't scared anymore. I was seriously PO'd. Someone had been tampering with my name, my computer, and—worse yet—my reputation. And I had a pretty good feeling I knew who she was.

With renewed determination, I walked out of my bedroom ready to fight. Ready to claw out the eyes of the imposter. It was only a matter of time before she exposed our identities, and that was totally unacceptable.

I crossed my living room, my sneakers squeaking against the wood floors. I loved that sound. Pacing the room, I began to formulate a plan. I knew the skirt would help!

Okay, first I was going to drive toward Chloe's neighborhood and see if there was a clear path to her room. Then I'd—

A shuffling sound behind me made my back go rigid. I paused at the edge of the kitchen and spied my car keys lying on the granite counter. Quickly I grabbed them, holding them between my knuckles as a weapon. I swallowed hard. Someone was here. I'd read about stranger danger in last month's *Cosmo*—

"Hey, baby."

"Aaiii!" I spun around, swinging my key weapon, striking out wildly. Aiden screamed back, obviously not expecting me to stab him in the ribs.

"Tess!"

"Frizzlesticks, Aiden! What are you doing here?" My heart was pounding out of my chest. Relief followed by giddiness at seeing Aiden were almost too much for me to handle. I dropped my car keys on the floor with a clank and to put my hands on his shoulders.

Aiden was bent over, holding his left side near his rib cage and looking up at me like *I* was the crazy one.

"Aw, fuck," he said quietly. "Am I bleeding?" He lifted up the side of his T-shirt, peering down at his chest.

Luckily he wasn't bleeding. But I glanced over his torso anyway, just to survey the damage. Okay, he was bleeding *a little*. I bit my lip guiltily.

"I am *so* sorry. You scared me and—"

"Tess," he said, sucking in a harsh breath. "Can you get me a bandage and an ice pack or something? It hurts."

I widened my eyes. "Oh. Right. Hang on." I dashed to the bathroom and rummaged through the medicine cabinet until I found my favorite pink Band-Aids with the strawberries. They were really cute. Just the sort of thing to cheer him up.

When I got back, I handed one to him with an apologetic smile. "They're scented," I told him. He rolled his eyes and handed it back.

"Can you please put it on for me? It's hard to see the spot where I was *stabbed*."

Sheesh. I'd already apologized. Besides, he had no idea what kind of pressure I'd been facing. Aiden pulled his T-shirt over his head, tossing it on the kitchen table, and stood there, bare-chested. Kind of sweaty. I breathed in deeply, loving that athletic smell.

I glanced up to meet his green-eyed stare.

"Like you haven't seen it before," he mumbled as he looked toward the ceiling with a huge grin.

I laughed, but it didn't stop me from taking a little longer than necessary (I was really concentrating on applying the adhesive). "There," I whispered, smoothing it down.

"Thank you, baby," he said, leaning in to kiss my cheek. "And hello. It's nice to see you. I have to say, I've definitely missed this uniform." He must have noticed the cleavage too.

"Sorry I assaulted you." I did feel awfully bad about that. "You just—"

"I know. I was trying to surprise you, not give you a heart attack. I stopped by the school to see Darren and bumped into Kira. She said you left early. I wanted to make sure you were okay."

"I'm just happy to see you. I called you a little while ago, but you didn't answer."

"Must have been on my way here," he said before walking over to the fridge. "Oh, yeah," he said, peering inside. "Your back door was unlocked. That's how I got in. Did you forget to lock it this morning?"

"What? It was? No." I looked toward the living room and furrowed my brow. I was 99.5 percent sure that I'd locked it before school.

Alarmed, I ran my fingers along the door frame. I gasped. Deep scratches.

"Aiden," I said, my voice trembling, "someone broke in

again!" My heart nearly exploded in my chest as I slammed and locked the door.

Jimmying open my lock was bad form. Sneaking in a window. Using a pick. All acceptable forms of breaking and entering. But actually damaging my property? Inexcusable. This copy-Kitten was either a complete rookie spy or thoroughly evil.

"Broke in?" Aiden asked. "What the hell do you mean, *again*?" He stomped over and protectively draped his arm around me. He was breathing heavily, as if he was ready to fight. He was still shirtless.

"Someone's been in your house?" His eyes were wide as he searched the room. "No wonder you're spazzing out, Tess. You should have told me." He exhaled. "Stay here. I need to make sure the house is safe."

"Safe?" I squeaked. It hadn't occurred to me that they could *still* be here. I'd just gotten dressed! What if some creepy stalker had been watching me? I sucked in a frightened breath.

Aiden took his hands from me, jetting his gaze around carefully until it landed on my mother's empty crystal candy dish from the side table. He lifted it above his head and slowly crept toward my room, looking decidedly dangerous.

I gulped. If someone was in my room, they'd need more than a strawberry Band-Aid once Aiden got done with them. My ex-boyfriend (sort of) was not about to let me get stalked. Um... again.

As I stood alone in my living room, all that registered was silence. But after a few minutes, my brain began to generate every horrible scenario imaginable. I couldn't wait any longer.

I walked toward my room, running my hand along the tan-painted wall to steady myself. "Aiden," I whispered. He didn't answer. I shouldn't feel this frightened. I'd been scaling trellises my entire high school career. But now I was acting like a scaredy-cat!

When I reached my half-closed door, I took a steadying breath. The hallway was silent, more silent than it should have been. As I slowly began to push open the door, I felt a tickle in my nose. I tried to wiggle it away, but it was too late.

I sneezed. A full-force, loud, bend-over sneeze. I knocked my forehead into my bedroom door and Aiden yelped as it banged into his back.

Then he dropped the crystal. There was a thunk (my head), a yelp (Aiden), and then the sound of glass breaking (loudly).

"Shit, Tessa!" Aiden yelled, holding his back where the doorknob had struck him. "I told you to wait!" He looked frustrated. Aiden's unexpected visit wasn't going all that well.

I reached up to feel my forehead. I was no longer scared, but definitely kind of sore. My forehead would no doubt be bruised after this little stunt. I couldn't believe that even in uniform, I could feel this discombobulated. "Ow," I said.

Aiden sighed, then stepped carefully around the broken shards of dish. He paused in front of me, reaching out to cup my face and tilt it up to him. "The room's clear," he said, his gorgeous green eyes shifting from my wound to my eyes. "But you've got a lump." He ran his finger over it gently. "And I have a stab wound."

I scrunched my nose. "Sorry."

"It's okay," he whispered, leaning over to kiss my shoulder, his fingers at the waistband of my skirt. "It just means that later, you're going to have to be nice to me. *Really* nice."

Heat rushed over me as I closed my eyes, letting Aiden wrap

me up in his arms. I had so much to talk to him about, but I didn't want to ruin the moment. I just wanted him.

I lay back into the soft chenille sofa with an ice pack on my head. After Aiden and I made out vigorously—working on our relationship—I realized that the bump on my head was totally killing me. Now he was being sweet—tending to my skull between bites of ice cream.

"So," I asked him as he spooned some Chunky Monkey into my mouth. "How did things go at school? Did you talk to Darren?" I let the bite slide down my throat, but I was still uneasy. I didn't know if Aiden had heard that SOS had been revealed, and I wasn't sure I was ready for him to know. He might go ballistic with worry.

"Yep," Aiden said, licking the back of the spoon before dipping back into the pint of ice cream. He glanced over at me. "Darren told me about SOS. That it's all over school. That some"—he held up finger quotes—"'crazy bitches' are spying on people." Aiden looked away and took a heaping spoonful of ice cream, chomping on it like he was mad. "What have you girls gotten yourselves into?" he asked, scooping more ice cream and holding it out to me.

I felt a familiar heat rise in my face, and I waved away the spoon. "Gosh darn it, Aiden! We haven't done anything."

He studied me, reading my reaction, before nodding. "I'm sorry," he said. "I didn't mean it like that. It was just hard hearing him describe you—or the old you—and pretending I knew nothing about it."

I pulled the ice off my forehead, feeling the onset of a headache. I was truly offended. I'd done everything I could to change my life, and it hurt that Aiden still didn't realize that. And it made me wonder if he'd been listening to me at all.

"I told you we've stopped spying," I murmured, sitting up to look at him. I left out the part about my pending investigation of Chloe. Aiden wasn't in the right frame of mind to hear about that.

He smiled, narrowing his eyes. "You also told me you quit cheerleading and, well..." He reached out and brushed at the hem of my skirt.

"I know this looks bad, but the girls need me." In more than just cheering.

He met my glare unapologetically. "It'll always be something, right, Tess?"

I wasn't sure what to think about us anymore. Obviously he hadn't gotten over his trust issues with me. Gosh, you tell one really big lie (for two years), and you never get trusted again. It was hardly fair. I'd said I was sorry.

We had been quiet for a few minutes when I heard my phone ring from the bedroom. It was good, something to break up the awkward party I was currently hosting on my couch.

"Do you want me to get it?" Aiden asked.

I struggled to stand up, but I was a little woozy. I must have hit my head harder than I'd thought. "If you wouldn't mind?"

He popped up off the couch and strolled toward my room, his long legs looking effortlessly agile in his track pants. I glanced at the clock on the cable box and saw that it was getting late. I needed to get ready for my surveillance, but I didn't want to be rude to Aiden. Ugh! I'd forgotten how hard it was to sneak around! I flopped onto the sofa and placed the ice pack over my forehead. Maybe I wasn't ready for this.

"Tessa," Aiden said, making me jump. I hadn't heard him come back. I looked up to see him standing above me. "It's Leona," he added, holding out the phone.

Oops. She probably wanted a status update…and I didn't have one. I sat up, feeling unsteady. When I had readjusted my position, Aiden put his hand over the receiver. "I'm sorry for being an asshole," he whispered.

I immediately perked up. "It's okay." I was ready to make up right now, even with Leona waiting on the phone.

"I just…" Aiden paused. He pressed his mouth into a smile and shook his head. "Never mind." He laughed. "We'll talk about it when you get off the phone."

Interesting. Completely set on telling Leona to call back later, much later, I pressed the phone to my ear. Aiden brushed his legs against mine as he moved past. I smiled, warmth spreading all over me.

I didn't want to waste any of our time together. Every day I felt us growing farther apart, and even the possibility made my insides ache. So without saying a word, I hung up the phone, leaned over, and kissed him.

ASSIGNMENT 2

10:30 P.M., SEPTEMBER 17

The operative rested her boots on the dash of her car as she lounged back, popping her gum. Typically Skinner Butte was full of steamed-up SUVs and Hondas, but tonight was quiet. Just a few people sitting on the cliff, watching the skyline. Her target hadn't arrived. This case was taking too long. She should have had a confirmation by now. The SOS files never showed a problem like this before. It was irritating.

She took out her phone, glancing through the messages, both her and the suspect's. Riley had been texting Megan since the moment she'd left the pizza place, but she wasn't responding. The operative wondered about this. Wondered if actively *not cheating* was still enough reason to keep investigating. She decided it was and readied her equipment.

A few minutes later, a black Ford F-250 pulled up to the butte. Immediately behind it was a red sedan with an open sunroof. Jenn.

They arrived just as they had arranged, and the operative knew that this would be it. This was definitely a cheat in progress; it had all the signs. As she scrambled to correct her seat, her elbow accidentally bumped the horn; the loud toot caused Jenn and Tate to jump from where they stood across the dirt hillside.

The operative froze in her spot, hoping that she hadn't just blown her cover. When Tate and Jenn turned back toward each other, she let out the breath she'd been holding. That was close.

There wasn't any way to get audio on this mission, so the operative grabbed the long-range camera from inside her pack. When the image was too dark, she switched it to night vision and let the green-hued figures come into focus.

The operative had been taking an online class on how to read lips, and she hoped to put her newfound skills to use. This was a time when words could be very incriminating. She zoomed in on Jenn's face and squinted.

"Tate," the operative mumbled as she read aloud. "We can't do this. It's not fair to Riley."

Tate shook his head, his dark hair hanging loose around his face. "I don't care about Riley. I care about you. I love you."

The operative swallowed hard but filmed the scene anyway, knowing that after the L word, a kiss was imminent.

Jenn closed her eyes and rubbed at her face before staring back at Tate. "I love U2," she mouthed.

U2? The band was great and all but...Oh. The operative widened her eyes and regained her composure. She knew it was only moments until lip lock.

"Come here," Tate said, taking Jenn by the wrists and pulling her to him. He wrapped her right up in his arms and rested his cheek on top of hers, facing the operative. "I'll wait as long as I need," he said. "I'll wait until you're ready."

"Damn it," the operative hissed. How had all the cheaters grown morals all of a sudden? It made her think of the guy she had cared about and how he—she paused. She wouldn't go there.

Figuring the night for a lost cause, the operative lowered

her camera and tucked it back into her bag. She watched for a few minutes as the couple sat together and admired the skyline. Her nail polish had begun flaking off. As much as she tried, she couldn't wrap her head around this assignment.

When people were in love, they weren't supposed to cheat. And Riley and Jenn claimed to love each other. *And* they claimed to love other people. In fact, Jenn and Megan were friends. What sort of friend did that? And what sort of girl loved two boys at once?

CHAPTER EIGHT

I WASN'T QUITE SURE HOW TO GET RID OF AIDEN.
The situation had gotten dicey when the phone rang three more times during our hookup, but I was in no position to answer it. Leona was probably furious. And now it was nearly dark, and my mission to dig into Chloe's extracurricular activities hadn't even started.

I wound up convincing Aiden that he'd beat traffic on the freeway if he left right then. When he finally agreed, I told him to call me when he got back to the Washington State campus. I nearly brought up visiting him there but chickened out at the last second. I really needed to consult *Cosmo* on how to handle this situation first.

Once Aiden was gone, I texted Leona to apologize for missing her call, blaming it on a bad connection. Then I told her I'd call her the minute I'd collected the surveillance. Her only reply was "whatever." Seemed that for me, spying and lying went hand in hand.

After deciding that being out in public in uniform—when I wasn't a cheerleader—might be a bit obvious for undercover work, I changed into loose-fitting jeans and a gray Wildcats T-shirt. It still inspired a little pep.

I drove the winding Redmond streets toward Chloe's father's

apartment in the old-town district. All the buildings here were nearly a hundred years old. Large porches, pastel exteriors— completely charming. Too bad none of that charm had worn off on Chloe.

It didn't take long to find her because the minute I pulled onto Harper Boulevard, she came barreling out of the double doors of a mint-green house on the corner. I had to slam on my brakes and veer over to avoid being seen. Wow. That was close. My heart was racing.

While I waited for her to pull out of her driveway, I checked my reflection. A small smile tugged at my lips. My face was flushed, giving me that bit of color I'd seemed to be lacking lately. Spying suited me. Too bad it left my insides in knots.

When Chloe left her street, I began following her, careful to keep at least three car lengths back. It was probably better that it was evening. The fading light helped to conceal my car color.

She pulled her Honda into a near-empty parking lot, and I did a double take. A bookstore? Really? I mean, I'd discovered long ago that the bookstore was an excellent pick-me-up when I was feeling down. Especially the romance section. But Chloe didn't strike me as the escapist type. Then again, she could be on an assignment of her own. Hm.

At least they had great coffee there—caramel Frappuccino (non-fat, of course)—and if I had a sec, I'd pick up a new mystery novel. It might take my mind off the real mystery that had become my life. I paused. I needed to refocus on this task. My mind was totally wandering! Very unprofessional.

I parked a row over and watched Chloe get out of her car, checking her reflection once in the side mirror. When she was inside, I pulled out my phone and texted Leona.

Target in sight. Bookstore.

She immediately answered. **Funny. Didn't know she could read.**

I snorted and shut my phone, slipping it into my pocket. I didn't have any official spy gear, but that was okay. I'd need to rely on my Kitten senses. In fact, this was the most alive I'd felt in weeks.

Careful to look casual and unnoticeable, I strolled toward the glass doors of the entrance. My intuition was telling me that Chloe was here as the copy-Kitten, but I'd have to catch her in the act. Maybe she was planting a listening device or conducting surveillance of her own. I narrowed my eyes and scoped the scene.

The well-lit store was complete with tall aisles of wooden bookcases that towered over me. The patterned maroon carpet had small pictures of coffee cups and pastries that pointed the way to the café in the back. My mouth was beginning to water.

Out of the corner of my eye, I saw a figure in black and immediately turned and headed for the first aisle, quickly grabbing a book and opening it to hide my face. When I felt like the coast was clear, I peered over the top of the binding.

Chloe was at the register, fingering through the bookmarks as she waited for a cashier. She didn't have anything else in her hands, so I figured she was going to ask a question. I twitched my nose. Maybe she wasn't here spying after all.

"Don't get that one." I jumped as someone spoke over my shoulder and lowered the book from my face. "The husband killed her for the insurance money. Totally obvious."

I spun around to see Joel there, toting a stack of books in his arms. He smiled, flashing that adorably crooked tooth of his. He was wearing a striped button-up shirt, and his brown hair was tousled expertly. He was dressed up, but in a not-really-trying sort of way. I glanced down at the lavender cover in my hands and then back at him. "What are you doing here?" I asked, still trying to catch my breath. "You scared the dickens out of me."

Joel stared, his mouth hanging open, then shook his head before reaching out to take my book. He set it on his stack, as though he planned to carry it for me. He was so chivalrous. "*Dickens?* Nice." He laughed.

"I thought you and Kira were having dinner tonight." I glanced back to see that Chloe was still at the register, talking to Jenn Duarte. Huh. Didn't know she worked here. After a quick chat, Chloe headed off to the Self-help section.

"We are," Joel said as I looked back at him. "But she was running late, so I'm just going to meet her at the restaurant." He tilted his chin toward the registers. "Check out?"

I wondered if Kira and Izzie were with Leona as I crossed the patterned carpet. When we got to the register, Joel set the books down with a thud. Jenn smiled her hello, her short brown hair tucked behind her ears. Then she began unstacking the books to ring them up.

"So what are *you* doing here?" Joel asked me. "I saw your ex-boyfriend at school today. Thought maybe he was in town to see you. You two back together?"

My lips parted, but no response came to me. Even though I'd just spent the last few hours making out with Aiden, I knew we were no closer to being back together. What was happening to my self-worth? Oprah would be ashamed! My eyes began to water.

"Oh, shit. Did I say something wrong?" Joel reached over to touch my wrist. I batted my eyes, trying to contain my tears. It seemed like I'd been crying more often than not these days.

"No," I said, my voice cracking. "I'm fine." But I wasn't. I felt…sort of trashy.

"Here," Joel said, leading me by the elbow over to the café. Books temporarily forgotten, I let him lead me forward over the cups and croissants embroidered in the carpet.

We stopped at a bar-height table, and Joel pulled the stool out for me, its legs screeching on the wood floor.

"Stay here," he said, looking worried.

I glanced out into the store but didn't see Chloe in between the stacks of books. She'd probably left, which meant I'd failed my mission. My spying capabilities had obviously gotten a little rusty. I sighed heavily and took a napkin from the table. I shredded it quickly, only to put it back together as a mini-pom-pom. I sniffled. I missed cheering!

I tried to control the new flood of tears that had begun to wash over me, but before I knew it, something frosty nudged my forearm. I looked up to find a Frappuccino in front of me and a smiling Joel sitting in the other chair with a large bag full of books.

"For me?" I asked, holding up the drink.

"Yep. You looked like a Frap girl. Vanilla, right?"

I took a sip, smiling down at the calorie-laden drink. "Caramel," I said between sips. "But this is pretty darn close."

Joel sipped from his coffee cup and glanced around the room before looking back at me. "Do you want to talk about why you just dissolved into a blubbery mess at the register?" he asked.

"No, thank you."

"Then we won't. Do you want to talk about the meeting you had with the principal?"

"Ick. Not really." I took a long sip from my drink, taking

comfort in the yummy goodness of the whipped cream. I sat up straighter and met Joel's kind stare.

Joel nodded as if truly considering something. "Fine," he said. "Then we'll talk about…" He paused and rubbed at his chin. "Fishing."

I smiled. "Fishing?"

"Yeah," he said, as if I was crazy to question the topic. "Fishing."

"With worms and hooks?"

"So you know of it?"

I opened my mouth, trying to figure out if he was serious or teasing me. He looked completely serious—not even a smirk. "Yes, Joel. I've heard of fishing. Even went a few times with my dad when I was little."

His mouth softened. "Really? Ever catch anything?"

"Not a thing."

"Wow." He shook his head. "You must have really sucked."

"Be quiet!"

"It's okay." He laughed, reaching out to pat my hand. "I'm sure it was the fishes' fault."

I leaned into the hard backrest, feeling decidedly less depressed, but I crossed my arms over my chest in mock anger and narrowed my eyes. "And how about you, know-it-all? How many fish have you caught?"

Joel's hazel eyes were amused. "Never been."

I gasped, and he sipped at his drink like he hadn't completely led me to believe he was a fish-catching expert. "Wow," I mocked, running my fingertip down the condensation on my cup. "You must have been really lame as a kid."

"Totally was," he said without missing a beat. "Read mystery novels and taught myself to play guitar while everyone else was impaling worms on hooks. Weird, huh?"

I started laughing just as a figure came into view behind Joel's shoulder. I gasped.

"Hey, Tess." Aiden walked up, his hands shifted in the pockets of his khakis. "Saw you sitting over here. Wanted to say hi."

My heart leapt from my chest as I ran my eyes over my favorite guy. "Hi," I answered. I'd thought Aiden left for campus a while ago. Maybe he stayed for me. Maybe he missed me!

Joel extended his hand to Aiden. "Hey, man," he said. Aiden nodded in greeting. "I should probably head out." Joel exhaled, motioning at his seat for Aiden as he stood up. Then he faced me, his expression soft. "Thanks for the talk, Tessa," he said. "And good luck hooking that fish."

I smiled, wrapping both hands around my nearly empty cup. After Joel walked away, Aiden plopped down across from me, but it was obvious something was wrong. His eyes were a little red and his T-shirt was wrinkled. I was suddenly filled with dread. Why did he look so upset? Especially when he'd stayed behind to look for me?

"You look positively dismal, Aiden. Is everything okay?" I reached over to put my icy fingers on his. He looked down and smiled weakly. When he finally lifted his head, he stared deep into my eyes. But rather than being comforting, his gaze was completely unsettling. There was something on his mind.

"Everything's all right," he finally said, squeezing my hand reassuringly. "I just wanted to make sure you're okay. When I saw you sitting here earlier...you just looked so sad. I couldn't leave you like that."

"Aww..." He really was sweet as honey.

"I—"

"Oh my God! A!"

My stomach twisted as Chloe Ferril came out from behind a bookshelf and beelined straight for my ex. Drats! She hadn't left after all. And now she was taking away my Aiden time. I might have growled under my breath.

"Uh…hey," Aiden said, looking back at me. I had just opened my mouth to talk when Chloe leaned in for a quick hug.

I tried not to let my blood boil over, seeing them together again. I had a lot of bad memories there. And it certainly didn't help that Chloe's red nails were clutching Aiden's tanned skin possessively.

"Hey, Tessa," she said without looking at me. Then she reached out to brush at Aiden's hair. "You look so grown," she cooed. "Oh, did you know that Mrs. Foster mentioned you in class the other day? It was so funny. She…"

The remains of my Frappuccino melted in my hand as I watched Chloe ramble on, obviously excited about Aiden's return. And even though she still looked gothy—black blouse, dark eyeliner, heavy boots—her cleavage had made a return. Hm…you'd think she'd known to expect him.

"Did you want to grab a coffee?" she asked him, motioning toward the barista. She glanced at the clearly empty drink in my hand but didn't invite me. The claws were about to come out.

It didn't matter if Aiden and I were technically broken up; he could not—absolutely not—drink any kind of beverage with Chloe. If he said yes to her, there might be a Kitten fight in here.

"Sorry," Aiden said, running a hand over his newly shortened hair, looking uncomfortable. "I have to head back up to school.

I was just stopping to see Tessa." Aiden looked at me and my stomach stopped twisting.

"Sure," Chloe said, tossing her long blonde hair over her shoulder. "Well, I guess I'll catch you next time you're in town. Talk to you soon."

She had started to walk toward the other side of the store when she paused and turned to me. "Hey, Tessa." She smiled broadly, looking proud to have touched my ex-boyfriend in front of me. "Could you stop following me now? You're really starting to creep me out."

I squeaked with surprise, nearly too stunned to answer. I could feel Aiden glaring at me as I nodded. For the first time, I'd been busted while spying. It was humiliating!

With that Chloe spun toward the exit doors, looking completely pleased with calling me out.

"So," Aiden said to me. I looked over, and he put his elbow on the table and rested his chin in his palm. "I'm not even going to ask what that was about."

"Good."

He shook his head. "You make me crazy, you know that, right? I couldn't keep you out of trouble even if I tried."

"Probably not," I agreed. My entire body was tense with the situation. I couldn't believe I'd been spotted. How was that possible? I'd been so careful.

"And you didn't have to growl," Aiden added. "I wasn't going to get coffee with her."

I laughed softly. So I actually growled? Even more embarrassing. "Aiden, you could have if you wanted. I'm not trying to hold you back." But I was just saying that to sound less needy. Fact was, I *was* trying to hold on to him.

Aiden twitched his mouth, staring down at the table. "About that." He paused, his green eyes not nearly as sparkly as before. "I was thinking…maybe you should consider dating a little. Other people, I mean."

My entire body went rigid. I couldn't respond; I just stared back at him, not moving.

"It's just," he continued, seeming to struggle with the words. "You're so unhappy, baby. And I know I'm the reason—"

"Are you seeing other people?" Please say no. Please say no. "No."

I exhaled, completely relieved. But I couldn't shake the stress rushing through me. "I don't want to see anyone else, Aiden," I whispered, trying to smile. "I like being with you."

He pressed his lips together, reaching out to run his index finger down the skin of my arm. "I like being with you too. Sorry I brought it up."

Well, glad that was settled. I would have pushed him to explain his thinking, or maybe the old Tessa would have, but I was completely stressed out. I needed to figure out (a) how to catch the copy-Kitten, (b) how to help the squad, and (c) what the hay was up with Aiden and me.

Aiden shifted in his seat. "All right, baby," he said as he stood up. "I have to take off. You going to be okay to get home?" He glanced over his shoulder toward the books and, for a second, I thought of Joel. How he tried to swoop in and save me from a complete public meltdown.

"Yes," I answered, climbing out of my chair to walk over and wrap my arms around Aiden's waist, resting my head on his chest. He sighed, twisting my ponytail in his hand, and then he let me go, leaving me a little chilly.

"I'll call you this week." He smiled and turned around to begin walking toward the exit. He didn't look back at me. Not once.

Slowly I began to cross the patterned carpet toward the glass doors at the front. Oh, wait. My book? I stopped, thinking about my lavender book and where I'd left it. I was about to go back to the checkout counter when something caught my eye.

I turned toward the figure leaving the store, her face ducked and her hands empty and without books. She was wearing a khaki skirt, and by the toned muscles in her legs, I was sure I knew her. I jogged after her, her thick brown hair pulled back into two short ponytails, her pink T-shirt tight enough to show off her athletic frame.

But the minute I was able to get out into the darkened parking lot of the bookstore, she was gone. I swung my head from side to side, looking for her, trying to remember what her car looked like, but she wasn't there. Neither was Aiden's car.

I narrowed my eyes, trying to figure out if she'd seen me and if she did, why she hadn't come over.

Because I was pretty sure that I'd just seen my ex-captain. I'd just seen Mary Rudick.

ASSIGNMENT 1

9:00 P.M., SEPTEMBER 18

The operative looked in her hand mirror and slicked on the Midnight Red lipstick that had become her personal trademark. When it was set, she pressed her lips together, smiling.

She'd been getting a ton of cases lately, but this one, this one was special. It was like watching the anatomy of a cheat—something that could easily be a *Dateline* investigation. She was privy to everything, and now, she just needed to catch the final act.

After slipping a black stocking cap over her head, the operative slid on leather gloves and watched the front of the motel intently. Originally she'd planned on tracking Jenn and Tate tonight, but then she'd intercepted a text from Megan. She'd asked Riley to meet her here, at the Sunset Inn at 9 p.m. She was still amazed that Megan would do that; from her observations, she'd seemed so much classier. Still, the operative knew that this was the moment she'd been waiting for. Finally.

She swallowed hard and narrowed her eyes, looking at the red-painted front door of the motel room. Riley had gone in there close to ten minutes ago, but the operative hadn't seen Megan arrive. She couldn't decide if Megan had beaten her there or if Riley was waiting.

With a sigh, the operative reached back into her car and grabbed her satchel. She'd filled it with the night-vision camcorder and an audio recorder, although she'd known it'd be difficult to hear much from outside.

As she strode across the loose gravel of the parking lot, the ground crunched under her black, high-heeled boots. The sound relaxed her and made her feel powerful, even in this cheater-filled world.

When she stepped onto the walkway in front of the door, she paused. The curtains were drawn tight; there was no way to get video. She narrowed her eyes.

Quietly she reached out to try the motel door, but it was locked. She'd figured it would be. With a glance toward the office window, she considered her next move. She pulled the knit hat off her head and shook out her hair. Armed with her deadly shade of red, her secret weapon, she made her way over to the management.

"Excuse me," she said sweetly through the Plexiglas window to the man inside. He smiled at her, his front tooth missing.

"Hey, there," he said, a little too friendly.

The operative smiled, trying to hide her revulsion. "I hate to bug you," she cooed. "I got locked out of room twelve, and my boyfriend must be in the shower because he's not answering. Do you think I could get another key?" She bit her lip suggestively.

At first, the dirty old man just watched her, but then he looked toward the walkway and smiled. "Okay, but make sure you turn in all the keys when you leave." He walked over to the key rack, taking a second to locate the peg numbered 12. When he turned back around, he grinned. "Tell your boyfriend he can thank me later."

The operative's stomach turned, but she tried to maintain a pleasant expression as she took the key. "Yeah, I'll let him know," she mumbled, turning back toward the room. She hated that this was taking so long, that it was so hard to confirm. She just wanted to make SOS successful. She wanted to be the best.

The operative stopped. No. This was about more than just her. Riley needed to learn that he couldn't dangle Megan along, and Megan needed to learn how to be a loyal friend. They couldn't just cheat with each other. They needed to be taught a lesson.

When she got to the room, the operative leaned her ear against the door and listened. She was disappointed to hear talking and not moaning. She couldn't complete her mission until they sealed the deal. But she could hardly break in with both suspects so alert. She chewed on the side of her lip and began to think. Then she smiled.

With purpose, the operative marched forward to the nearest fire alarm, glancing around once to make sure no one could see her. When she was certain the coast was clear, she slipped her fingers around the little white handle…and yanked it down.

Sirens filled the air, and the operative moved quickly toward her car, ready to grab her camera. Seeing Riley and Megan run out in their underwear (or less) would be all the proof she needed, especially given their location.

The operative ran across the lot, her boots crunching on the gravel. She slipped into the front seat of her car, grabbing her zoom lens and aiming it at the red door just in time.

Within seconds, the door swung open, and Riley popped his head out to look around. The operative clicked off a few pictures, stopping only when Riley opened the door the rest of the way.

He was fully dressed. Behind him, Megan walked out, looking confused. And she was dressed too. As a maid (a real one).

"Shit," the operative mumbled, lowering her camera. This was where Megan worked, not a steamy late-night rendezvous. Megan and Riley headed toward the glass window of the office, apparently intending to ask about the alarm.

That was the operative's cue to get the hell out of there. Once again, she didn't have proof. And now it was really starting to piss her off.

CHAPTER NINE

AS I GLANCED AROUND THE BOOKSTORE PARKING
lot for Mary's car, I pulled my pink phone from my jeans pocket,
hesitating only as I remembered that Aiden didn't own a cell. It
had never really bothered me when we were dating, but then again,
we'd been attached at the hip. Or lips. Whichever was closer.

I got to my car and sped away from the store, my mind twisting
around the situation. *Mary Rudick?* What was she doing in town,
and why would she come here without calling me? Something was
suspicious about that. I'd need to consult the squad.

Call me ASAP!! I sent out a multiple text to Leona, Kira,
and Izzie. Nearly five minutes went by without an answer. Dang it!
Where were they?

I tossed my phone onto the seat, pressing a little harder on the
accelerator as I climbed the hills toward my house. My insides
turned with uneasiness, all stemming from my experience at the
bookstore. And that was terrible. It used to be a safe place.

When I pulled into my driveway, the headlights illuminated
the wood siding on my house. My parents still weren't home. For
a second, I thought about the break-in and how I'd be vulnerable
alone. But then I pictured Mary Rudick and how she had bolted
out of that store. What did it mean? I couldn't waste time sitting in
my car, scared. I needed to get to the bottom of this.

As soon as I got inside, I locked the door and dialed up Kira. She didn't answer, and I remembered that she was meeting Joel for dinner. Hm. I didn't want to involve too many Kittens. This was top-secret stuff.

I decided to try Leona, only *her* line went directly to voice mail. I hung up without leaving a message and began to pace my living room. Izzie's mother told me that she was out with her "good-for-nothing" boyfriend, and Aiden's dorm voice mail was too full to take messages. I felt lost. Completely alone.

I collapsed on the couch and flipped channels, spotting an ad for a psychic hotline. "Secrets exposed." I wondered if Madame Corrine would be able to tell me the identity of the copy-Kitten. Well, it was worth a shot. I was just about to dial her number for the free trial when my phone vibrated in my hand.

It was an unfamiliar number. "Hello?"

"Hey, Tess. It's Joel. Sorry to call you so late. I—"

"Joel? How did you get my number?" I clicked off the TV and sank back into the sofa cushions. I was just happy to have someone to talk to.

"Oh...I, um, I got it from Kira's phone earlier."

I furrowed my brow. "You're not still with her?"

"No." He exhaled. "She said she was tired and that she'd grabbed something to eat with Leona earlier."

"Rude," I said, before I caught myself. "Sorry. I didn't mean it like that."

"No worries," Joel said, his voice quiet. "You're right." He paused and cleared his throat. "Actually, Tessa. I was wondering if you were up for giving advice? You have...a unique outlook on life." He chuckled and I wasn't sure if he was complimenting me but decided he was too nice for veiled insults.

"Thanks, it's sweet of you to say." I sat up, my bare feet pressing against the floor. "But is everything all right?"

Joel let out a sad laugh. "I don't think so," he said.

My lips pouted. He sounded so melancholy. "Hey," I said. "My parents are late getting home, and I haven't had anything to eat. If you want to come by, I can order a pizza or something. I have a coupon." Truth was, right about now, I could use a friend too.

"That sounds perfect," he said, sounding relieved. "And thrifty! See you soon."

After the pepperoni (his half) and pineapple (my half) pizza arrived, Joel and I ate at the coffee table while watching some super-lame documentary on the solar system. It was sort of funny, considering the earlier mix-up about outer space he and Kira had had. But when I pointed it out, he didn't seem to get the humor.

"Ugh," I said, sinking to the floor and leaning my back against the couch. "I'm so full."

"Probably shouldn't have inhaled half a pizza, then."

I snapped my head back to Joel, who laughed. "I'm joking, Tess! I mean, sure, it wasn't as funny as your solar system joke." He rolled his eyes. "But still a joke."

I smiled and closed up the empty box, setting our plates on top. Then I climbed up to sit across from him on the couch. It was time to get down to business. "So," I said. "What did you want to talk about?"

Joel flinched, almost like he was hoping I wouldn't bring it up.

"I feel stupid now," he said, closing his eyes. "I shouldn't be bothering you with this stuff. You have your own problems."

I sure did.

"But it's Kira. I...I don't know what's going on with us." When Joel's soft hazel eyes met mine, I could see how sad he was. He truly cared about Kira. What was her deal? Didn't she know how hard love was to come by these days? She was totally fouling out!

I rested my head against the back of the sofa, thinking. "What happened tonight?" I asked.

He exhaled. "Well, we were supposed to meet for dinner. Then she shows up late, all frazzled, and says that her cheers were completely 'effed' and that she had to meet with Leona tonight to go over them."

The pineapples turned in my stomach. The squad was continuing to leave me out. I felt my own eyes sting with tears.

"So I asked her if she wanted to grab something from the drive-through, and she tells me she's already eaten! I mean, I was waiting for her, Tessa!" Joel's voice took on an edge, and to be honest, it was kind of hot. It was a real moment—a moment where you could see someone's passion. I blinked heavily.

"Tessa?" he asked softly, meeting my stare. "Do...do you think she's cheating on me?"

Fudge ripple! Was he serious? "No way! Kittens don't cheat!"

Joel tilted his head in complete confusion. "Uh . . . *okay*. Is that like part of your cheerleader pledge or something?"

Right. I sometimes forgot that people didn't know we were SOS. "Yes," I said confidently. "And Kira's been through a lot. With a lot of guys." Joel looked a little sick.

Oops. I also sometimes forgot that not everyone knew about Kira's promiscuous past.

"What I mean is..." I paused, not wanting to do any more damage. I sighed. "She loves you," I said simply. "She just does."

I smiled. "And I can see why. You're an awfully nice guy, Joel. Kira's a lucky girl, and she's not likely to forget it." There. That sounded much better.

Joel watched me carefully, his crooked tooth peeking out just a little beneath his parted lips. It was his little quirks—the tooth, the T-shirts, the...non-fishing—that made him that little bit of extra cool. "And you're a nice girl too," he said. "Despite what they say."

"What?" My heart jumped in my throat.

"I'm kidding," he said, laughing. "Wow, Tessa. You really need to work on your sense of sarcasm."

I didn't tell him that I found sarcasm rude.

"God," he said, glancing down at the shiny silver watch on his arm. "It's getting late. I should go."

"Oh." I was disappointed. I liked having the company.

He paused as he stood. "Unless there was something you wanted to talk about?"

Joel was such a mind reader! There was a lot I needed to talk about, but most of it was top secret. No. I needed to talk the Mary thing over with the squad, and only the squad. Or at least, I would if they ever decided to let me in their loop again.

"I'm fine," I said, standing up to walk him out. "But I'll let you know if something comes up."

Joel looked down at me, narrowing his eyes. "You're a mysterious girl, Tessa Crimson. And very interesting. I hope your boyfriend comes to his senses soon."

"Thanks." I wished he would too.

As Joel and I crossed the living room into the kitchen, he snapped his fingers. "Wait, I almost forgot!"

"What?" I looked at the sofa but didn't see anything.

"I'll be right back," he said, jogging quickly out the front door.

I peeked out the front-hall window to see Joel reach in the passenger side of his car, light up its interior, and grab something on the floor. Then he slammed the door shut and ran back over to me.

"For you," he said, extending a small, square package in one arm. I looked down, and my stomach fluttered.

"My book?" It was the lavender-covered mystery novel!

"Yep. You left it on my pile of novels, so I bought it for you. You were sort of a blubbery mess."

I blinked, turning the book over in my hands, and then glanced at him. "Thank you." An overwhelming mix of feeling rushed through me. I wanted to both laugh and cry because at that moment, I felt special. Not invisible.

"Anytime," Joel said quietly, giving me a smile as he backed slowly toward his car. "I'll talk with you again soon, okay?"

I nodded, waving once to him. I liked Joel. In fact, he might be exactly the sort of friend I needed right now. Someone that didn't judge me. Didn't—

My cell phone vibrated in my pocket, making me jump. I moved back inside the house, turning the dead bolt on my front door before pulling out my phone. It was Kira.

"Hey," I said, exhaling. "I've been trying to call you."

"I saw that. Sorry. Hey, I'm just around the corner at Taco Bell with Leona and Izzie. Can we stop by?"

"Oh." I suddenly wondered if Kira knew that her boyfriend had just left my house, but I didn't think so. It wasn't like we were doing anything wrong. Still. I might want to keep it to myself. "Sure," I said finally. "I have to talk to you about something anyway." I wondered what they would think of Mary being in town.

"Perfect," she said. "See you soon."

When she hung up, I stood in the hallway, feeling a bit uneasy. Something about her clipped tone made me wonder what exactly had happened tonight. I swallowed hard. I needed some confidence. I needed...the skirt.

(CODE PINK) SOS
INTER-KITTEN COMMUNICATION

Dear Smitten Kittens,

Due to recent events, all of our inter-Kitten communication will change to our most top-secret status: Code Pink.

We are formulating a plan to combat the heinous rumors surrounding the outing of SOS. None of us were involved in the rogue messages or the inefficiently designed blog. It was an imposter.

While we finish assessing the damage, do not discuss SOS with anyone outside the group. There is still a chance for us to remain anonymous.

If you have any questions, please use the Code Pink hotline at 555-0101. Do NOT make any communications on the SOS database or e-mail lines.

Keep smiling,

Leona ☺

CHAPTER TEN

LESS THAN FIVE MINUTES LATER, MY DOORBELL
rang. When I opened it, Izzie looked me over and squealed at the sight of my uniform. Kira touched her throat, speechless, I guessed. Leona rolled her eyes behind her glasses (still decked out in her own greasy cheer skirt).

"Playing dress up?" she asked with a smile, glancing down at my uniform as she walked past me into the house.

It may have seemed odd that I was in uniform, but I was sure they understood. We all suffered from the same spirit addiction.

"I like your glasses," I said to Leona. They were the hip, beehive ones with a thin silver chain. They made her look delish.

"I knew it was time to get serious," she said, motioning me over to the kitchen table. "And that meant it was time to accessorize."

I was glad we were all confronting the realities of the situation. I hoped they'd been as focused at their practice. When I sat down on the cold wood of my kitchen chair, Kira looked me over.

"Are...are you wanting to rejoin the squad?" she asked. "Because we'd need to have a vote first, and I'm not sure you have the support yet."

"What?" I asked, my face stinging. "No, I wasn't going to rejoin the squad. I just wanted to wear the uniform. But—"

"Surprised it still fits," Leona mumbled, tapping her nails on the tablecloth.

I looked at her and then back at Kira. "What did you mean, 'not sure I'd have the support'? Are you saying some of the Kittens would vote against me? I was their captain for—"

"Well, I think you look hot," Izzie remarked, ignoring my conversation as she combed her fingers through her red hair. "Makes your boobs look *huge*."

"Hey!" I said loudly, slapping my hand on the table. The girls jumped and then stared at me, wide-eyed. "Are you saying I can't rejoin the squad?" Up until just then, I hadn't realized just how badly I wanted to be a Smitten Kitten again. But now I wanted it. It was my rightful place, and how dare they not let me cheer! I had fabulous routines!

Kira and Izzie exchanged a nervous look, and Leona leaned back in the kitchen chair. "Don't be alarmed," she started. Immediately my bells and whistles went off. "But I talked to Mary Rudick."

"Speaking of," I said. "I saw her tonight!"

They didn't flinch. Wait. Why didn't they look surprised?

I pulled my eyebrows together. "Did you know she was in town?" Goose bumps broke across my arms.

Kira nodded. "She came to practice tonight."

What in the world? "Why would she do that?"

"She was concerned," Kira spoke up. "About you. Said she thought you'd want to rejoin the squad but that you weren't ready. She said your activities with Aiden had compromised you and that we shouldn't take you back. She gave a pretty good speech. I think she swayed a few of the girls her way."

"She said that?" My breath felt caught in my chest. I might hyperventilate.

"She was kind of bitchy tonight," Leona added, rubbing the pad of her index finger over her front teeth to remove any lingering lipstick. "Total rag."

"I didn't think she was that bad," Izzie said, looking between them. She must have noticed the devastation on my face because she winced. "I mean, other than the not letting you be a Smitten Kitten again thing."

My eyes were stinging, and I couldn't stop a few tears from falling. In a million years, I never thought a fellow Kitten would betray me. We were like family. I had an idea of how my life looked to other people, and it wasn't great. I knew that things weren't perfect anymore. But I'd been learning to be okay with it. Until now.

"Is this why you're here?" I asked, meeting Kira's eyes. She tried to smile supportively at me, but behind her expression she looked upset. "To tell me I can never cheer again?"

Kira's face scrunched. "Heck no, Tessa," she said. "We're here to help you get *back* on the squad."

My heart leapt. "Good gravy, K." I sighed, reaching out to hug her. "You must have read my mind. I could use some positive perk right about now."

"Perfect! So you'll come to the movies with us tomorrow?"

I straightened up. "Movies?" I looked at Izzie and Leona, and they both glanced away like they knew this was coming. "How will that get me back on the squad?"

Kira pressed her lips together. I felt small. Kira had never made me feel so insignificant before. "I know you're ready to get to business—cheering, spying—all that," she said. "But first, we need to work on your image. Mary addressed the squad about it tonight. And to combat what she said, we need to show that you're up to snuff, Tess. You need to pull yourself together."

"My image?" I looked down at my uniform. Sure, it was a little tight, but hardly unbecoming.

"Not physically," Kira pointed out.

"Maybe a little," Leona muttered. I narrowed my eyes at her.

"What I mean to say is…" Kira was fumbling with her words. I knew from experience that usually meant she was trying to be nice. "Your reputation has taken a bit of a stomping since last year. I think before you campaign for the vote, you should have a…coming-out party."

"Oh my word!" Izzie gasped, turning to me. "You're gay? I thought this was because the guys at school are calling you slutty."

Slutty? I wasn't used to a word like that being associated with me. "I'm straight," I said to Izzie. "And I'm certainly not…that other word." I turned to Kira. "Is that really what they're saying, K?" After years of being a great example, I was getting treated terribly. It wasn't fair!

Kira gnawed on her lip, unable to meet my eyes. Then she nodded.

Well, she might as well have slapped my face because I felt sacked. How quickly a school can turn against you! Even your own squad. "So…are you telling me that I need to fix my reputation before you'll let me cheer?"

Leona reached out and patted my hand. "I think under the current circumstances, we need to resurrect our image. And it's going to start with you."

I sniffled, feeling my nose beginning to run. "I'm an embarrassment."

"Don't think of it that way," Leona said, leaning over to wrap
one arm over my shoulders. "We love you, Tess. You're our true
captain." Kira shifted next to me. "We just feel like some damage
control might be in order."

I was flabbergasted. Totally deflated. I could have told them
that Principal Pelli had practically given me the squad earlier,
but what would that solve? Obviously the Smitten Kittens had
their doubts about me now. I half wondered if they thought *I* was
the copy-Kitten. I sighed, feeling nauseous and not at all perky.
"What did you have in mind?" I asked.

"A movie," Kira said, sounding happy that I'd asked. Leona
straightened up and took out a pocket mirror before retouching
her lipstick.

"And how will that help?" My face was hot with humiliation.
I was at their mercy now. I felt like I'd fallen from atop the human
pyramid.

Kira took me by the droopy shoulders and turned me to face
her. "Being single," she began, "is not working for you. At all."

Ouch! That was a low blow.

"And I know you still love Aiden," she added quickly, reading
my expression. "But that car has sailed. He—"

"It's ship."

"Right. Well, either way, he's in college, and you guys aren't
really dating anymore. Not officially. And although I know that's
completely tragic, it's time for you move on. But"—she held up
a finger in warning—"you need to move on with the right type of
guy."

"Type?" I'd never dated anyone other than Aiden. Did I have a type?

"Now, tomorrow night Joel and I are going to a movie, and I decided that you should come with."

She was making less sense by the moment. "I still don't see how that's going to help."

"Double date!" she squealed like it was the best idea she'd ever heard. "We've decided—Chris Townsend is perfect for you. He's totally sweet and he has a great rep."

"He is nice," Izzie agreed. "And I might bring Sam. So it'll be a triple date."

"It's called a trilogy." Kira shook her head. "Leona? Did you want to tag along? I'm sure Joel can find a friend for you."

"Ew," Leona snapped, taking off her glasses to glare at Kira. "I don't need you to set me up. I'm not desperate."

"Hello," I said, raising my hand. "Neither am I."

The table got quiet. I looked around at all the girls, wondering if they did think I was desperate. Sure, maybe I was hooking up with Aiden while we weren't technically together, but who wouldn't? He was adorable.

I looked between them, feeling my lips pull into a pout. For the first time, being in the skirt wasn't making me feel better. It was making me feel bad about myself.

Then I remembered that even Aiden suggested that I date other people. Golly, I must look really pathetic—to everyone. I lowered my head. Maybe Aiden was right. Then again, maybe if I did this double date thing and got back on the squad, I'd be perk-perfect again. Then Aiden would see that I didn't need anyone else. He'd want me back. Officially.

"Fine," I said. "I'll go to the movies. But it's just for show—not a real date. I still think there's a chance for Aiden and me. I'm not ready to move on."

"Knowing is the battle," Kira said, beaming.

"It's half the battle," I corrected.

She rolled her eyes. "I was being optimistic."

I tried to swallow, but my throat was too dry. I looked back toward my fridge, wishing I had the energy to get a glass of water. Being told that you needed to date against your will to get back on the cheer squad would exhaust anyone.

"Well, that was a fun conversation, Kira," Leona scoffed from the other side of the table. "Now that it's settled, let's get to the real topic. What was the deal with Chloe tonight? Seriously. A bookstore?" She snorted.

"I'm not sure it's her anymore," I said, trying to refocus. "She caught me following her and—"

"Wait," Kira interrupted. "You got caught? That's never happened before!"

"I know." I nodded. "And then on top of that, while I was there, I saw Mary. And I'm telling you girls, she was acting really strange."

"Interesting," Leona said, leaning back in her chair and crossing her arms over her chest. "Could be because she was about to try to get you blackballed from the squad. But then again, she could be the copy-Kitten."

"No way," Izzie said. "Mary is way too savvy to be the copy-Kitten. Whoever's impersonating us is dumb."

"Who says?" Kira sat up. "I bet they're super-smart. Like a techie or something. Or," she added, holding up her finger, "she could be someone desperate for attention." They all looked at me.

I watched them for a minute before we all looked down at the table. Seemed like none of us really was above suspicion. Leona sighed next to me.

"God. What if it's really a mass murderer or something?"

Izzie squeaked. "Murderer?" I looked across at her as she bit her red nails. Her eyes darted around the room. "Would they kill cheerleaders?"

"No," I said, trying to comfort her. "I'm sure they don't kill anyone, especially not cheerleaders."

"Nah. My money is still on Chloe," Leona said. "She's totally mental and clearly still obsessed with Aiden."

"And what about Christian?" Kira spoke up. "Even though he's not around, it could still be him." She smiled to herself. "It's actually kind of hot to think of him peeking in my window at night."

"Ew," Leona snapped. "It is not. It's pervish and illegal. Quit being such a freak, Kira."

"Quit being such a b-i-t-c-h, *Leona*!" Kira shot back.

As they began to trade insults, I looked across the table at Izzie. She was petrified, poor thing. The arguing was certainly not helping her self-esteem issues. And I'd heard her position on the soccer team might even be in jeopardy. I had to take control of this situation.

"Enough," I said sternly, waiting for them to stop. To my surprise, they did. Guess I did still have a little power after all.

"Do you have a plan?" Kira asked. I wondered if she'd been waiting for me to come up with one all along.

"Not really. But I do think it's time for us to get serious and re-form SOS—the real one. This assignment is too big for just one Kitten." I paused and looked between them. "Unless I'm not allowed to spy, either."

All three girls looked down at the table, avoiding my eyes. "Of course you can help with SOS," Kira murmured before glancing up.

I smiled a little. Suddenly I felt better. Like I'd just regained a small piece of myself. "Okay, then. Let's get the entire squad together after school tomorrow and fill them in."

I hated breaking promises. And right now, I'd just broken (another) promise to Aiden. I wouldn't tell him about SOS. I couldn't. Not when our relationship was already so strained. Or, as some would call it, nonexistent. And I'd probably leave out the part where I go on a date with Chris Townsend. He was just a decoy anyway.

"About time," Leona mumbled. "We should have never stopped SOS in the first place."

I shot a glance at her, but she wasn't looking at me. She was biting her thumbnail. I blinked quickly, then touched her forearm. "Do you think you can start drafting up a timeline of the events so far?"

"Yep." She sighed before getting up. She put on her glasses and smiled at me. I could tell she was happy that we were all going to spy again. I think she missed the excitement. "It'll give me something to do since there's no routine to memorize. Kira blew another practice."

"Did not! I wasn't exactly expecting Mary Rudick to show up."

I widened my eyes. "So no routine?" I asked. Homecoming was only a few short weeks away. Principal Pelli was going to have a coronary!

"Look, Tess," Kira snapped. "I'm trying, okay? Get off my back."

I gasped, staring at her. It was completely unlike her to be rude. Outbursts like that were generally reserved for Leona. "I didn't mean—"

"No." She shook her head. "I'm sorry. I'm just super-stressed."

I completely understood. The stress had sent me into near PTSOSD last year. "I believe in you, K," I whispered encouragingly. She looked sideways at me. And smiled.

"Thanks. I needed to hear that."

We all sat quietly until Leona stood up, yawning and reaching her arms above her head. "Fun stuff, girls. But I need to take off."

"Me too," Izzie added. "Sam's coming by later for ice cream."

We set up to meet tomorrow, and after the Kittens scattered, I grabbed my cell from over near the couch and scrolled through the missed calls. When I found what I was looking for—Mary Rudick's number—I dialed.

"*Ding, ding, diiiiiing*. Sorry, the number you are trying to call has been disconnected—"

Interesting.

(CODE PINK) SOS
INTER-KITTEN COMMUNICATION

Dear Smitten Kittens,

I have put together the first mission in Operation Knockoff. (Because we all know this copy-Kitten is a cheapened version of the real SOS.) Please read below for your assignment, and then sign off and return the form to me ASAP.

Kira—visit the scenes of the cheats we know the copy-Kitten investigated and see if there's any evidence that might point to a culprit. Cigarette butts, shoe imprints…think *CSI*.

Izzie—hack into the county database and see if any tickets were issued around the times of the incidents involving the fake SOS.

Tessa—use your power of super-sleuthing and try to talk to some of the guys on the posted Naughty List to see if they noticed anything irregular or out of place. They may tell you more if you wear that red lipstick I let you borrow—it looks fabulous on you!

Everyone else, be on the lookout. There are plenty of rumors floating around. I'll be conducting some research on recent entries or exits from the school population, looking for any obvious suspects.

If you have any questions, please use the Code Pink hotline at 555-0101. Do NOT make any communications on the SOS database or e-mail lines.

Keep smiling,

Leona ☺

Sign_____Date_____

CHAPTER ELEVEN

"HEY, PUMPKIN," MY FATHER CALLED AS HE WALKED in the front door. It was close to midnight and I was still in my uniform, lying on the couch. "Your mother had to run to the corner store for some milk. Apparently we're out."

"Dad?" I looked at him, feeling a little lost. It would be good to have my parents back home. I hadn't seen them much lately, what with all the gigs, and I missed them. Besides, I hated being alone in the house after the recent break-ins. In the last few hours (at least I thought it'd been a few hours) I'd considered all the possible reasons that Aiden and I weren't back together. Why he brought up me dating other guys. I had only one conclusion: another girl.

"You feeling okay?" my father asked, settling next to me on the couch. He took off his glasses and looked me over carefully. "You're...in uniform."

"I know." I dropped my head. "I was feeling down, and maroon and gray always cheer me up. Principal Pelli called me into the office and actually suggested that I rejoin the squad. He thought it would be best."

"That's great!" My father looked ecstatic. I think he and my mom missed making signs to hold up at the games. "Are you and Kira co-captains?"

My stomach turned. "Not...quite."

He folded up his glasses and tucked them into the front pocket of his shirt. "I don't understand. Are you and the Smitten Kittens having problems?"

"They won't let me rejoin. They want me to date someone else first," I blurted out, needing him to confirm that they had cartwheeled their way to crazy.

"Not let you join? But..." He exhaled, seeming to consider this. My father frowned, weighing his words. "Well, maybe they're right." He waited. I blinked and stared back at him.

"Didn't you hear me?" Obviously I wasn't communicating very well. "They want me to date someone *other* than Aiden."

My father scratched at his chin stubble. "But you and Aiden aren't dating anymore, right? I thought you two were just friends."

Although I hadn't really explained the situation to my father in full, I still felt like I'd just been slapped in the face. Hadn't he seen how hard I'd been working to improve myself? To win Aiden back?

"Honey," he said, lowering his head. "I know how much you care for Aiden. And you know your mom and I adore him too. But..." He trailed off. "You're a smart girl, Tessa," he finished. "And I'm not going to tell you what's best for you. Because you already know."

He rose from the couch, bending down only to kiss the top of my head before wandering off to the kitchen. I didn't move for a while after he left. I sat there on the couch staring at the place where my skirt ended and my thigh began. I stared at it until the first tear dropped onto my lap and the rest blurred my vision altogether.

* * *

After my long-overdue cry fest, I made my way to my room for a nap. A little beauty sleep couldn't hurt. But it felt like only seconds after I'd closed my eyes when my phone vibrated on my bedside table. I rolled over and picked it up, glancing at the screen. Another unfamiliar number. Strange.

I clicked it on and put it to my ear. "Hello?" I asked, my voice kind of scratchy.

"Tessa? It's Mary. We need to chat."

My heart nearly stopped. "Mary?" I squeaked.

"I know you're probably PO'd," she said. "But understand, I've been hearing some pretty disturbing things."

I sat up in my bed, needing to clear my head for the impending conversation. "I'll be honest," I said before clicking on the pink porcelain lamp on my side table. "I am very ticked at you, Mary. I'd like to know exactly why you went behind my back like that?" My fingers were shaking from the confrontation.

She exhaled. "I tried to call you first, remember? Then...when I didn't hear from you, I decided to take things into my own hands. You've been completely out of control lately. And when you said you were going to see the principal, I just about guessed what it was for. That man is nothing if not predictable. But you're not ready to take back the throne, Tessa. You can't even keep your personal life in order, let alone your professional one."

I was truly offended. What did she know of my personal life? "You completely crossed the line," I said, my voice low. "I want back on the squad, Mary. And it's not your place to keep me away."

She laughed. "Don't make this personal. I'm doing what's best for the Smitten Kittens. Did you think I wouldn't find out how badly you effed up SOS? I trusted you with my organization. It means something, Tessa! It's my legacy."

"SOS was misguided and wrong. I was trying to let us all move on."

"No," she said. "*You* were trying to move on."

That was it. I was done with this conversation. "Mary, not only are you not in charge of the squad anymore, you're not even on it. You don't have a vote. Not there and not in my life. So I'd appreciate it if you stepped away from the situation. Kira and I have it handled."

"Kira," Mary said, fighting to control her voice. "Can't believe you made her captain."

I'd never told Kira, but Mary had always been against letting her join the squad. She didn't feel that she had the right image, the right oomph. But I thought Mary was being completely judgmental. And now she was turning her judgment on me. "I have to go," I said finally. "We'll handle our own squad and the fragments of SOS."

"Is there some drama between you and Kira?" she asked.

"No," I answered, maybe a little too quickly.

She laughed. "Fine. But just so you know, tension often occurs when there's a shift in power. Keep it in mind."

"I will," I murmured, considering her comment. "'Night."

She hung up without a reply, and I pulled the phone slowly from my ear, staring at it. Of all people, I never thought I'd have to go sneaker to sneaker with my ex-captain. And even though something like this would have totally hurt the old Tessa's feelings, the new me...was just furious. I'd show Mary Rudick.

I curled up on my side, considering her words. Had Kira changed because of her new position? It seemed unlikely.

But before recently, Kira had never shown me even a tinge of animosity.

Then again, maybe Leona was right. Maybe Kira was on a big power trip. I needed to talk to Aiden.

I grabbed my phone and quickly dialed, but Aiden's dorm phone went straight to voice mail. It made me sad, or at least it did until I saw the copy of my new book sitting where I'd left it on my nightstand. It had been undeniably sweet of Joel to bring it to me earlier. I felt myself smiling as I thought of it.

I opened the front cover, and a note I hadn't noticed before caught my eye:

If you need to talk or just want to relive old fishing stories, call anytime. Joel, 555-6872.

I laughed, closing the cover and clicking off the light before settling back into my bed. I considered calling to thank him. Maybe even chat a little. But to be honest, most of my problems were top secret. And I didn't think it was best to fill him in on my (or his girlfriend's) spying past. No. Joel was great and all, but there were some things a Kitten needed to handle on her own. Like finding the person who was impersonating her.

And with that, I snuggled under my covers, hugging the book to my chest, and closed my eyes.

When I woke up the next morning, my parents were still in their room, sleeping off last night's gig. I quietly made my way through the house as I began to fill with dread at the thought of the impending day.

I sat down with my cereal, crunching it with little vigor, and decided to try Kira. She picked up on the first ring. Someone to talk to!

"Morning, Tess," she said, and yawned. "You just caught me. I was just about to start working on some cheers for homecoming. What's up?"

"Oh," I said. "Did you want some help?"

I heard the phone shift like Kira was just getting out of bed, which she most likely was. "Um…maybe next time, okay? Let's get through your date first."

My smile faded as I put down my spoon. I'd forgotten that I didn't have a place on the squad yet. It was another crushing blow. "Sure. Next time."

"Perfect," she said. "So, we're still on for the movies tonight, right? I've already e-mailed Chris, and he is oh-so-excited to hang out with you. That boy is over the sun for you!"

"It's the moon."

"He's not a werewolf." Kira laughed. "I doubt the moon has anything to do with it. But wait until he sees you in uniform again. He'll be howling, all right."

"Oh my word." I grinned, spooning cereal into my mouth as I considered the evening ahead. "I don't know about tonight, K," I answered. "Dating someone other than Aiden sounds completely dull. Can we just focus on the investigation and get it over with?" I pushed away my bowl and rested my elbows on my kitchen table.

"This is part of the investigation. Getting you back up to snuff is just as important as finding the copy-Kitten. Once they see that you're on your game, Tess, they'll chill out. I just know it."

In a way, I knew she was right. On paper, Chris was my perfect match. I should try to focus on that. Because I also knew that you couldn't rush a Smitten Kitten induction. Even though I had already been an important member of the squad, I needed to earn my pom-poms back.

"Oh," Kira said. "I've got another call." There was a pause, then she was back. "Darn, it's Izzie. She's got some major boyfriend drama going on. I'll talk to you later, okay?"

I was suddenly jealous that Izzie would call Kira with a problem before me, but then I reminded myself that Kira was captain and, therefore, the go-to Kitten.

"Yeah, I'll be around. Call me later."

"Actually, Tess, can I talk to you at school? Leona and Izzie are on their way over."

My muscle flinched. "For what?"

"My routine." She paused. "I guess if you wanted to come by and watch, that would be okay. Do you want to?" She felt sorry for me.

I was hurt that she hadn't asked sooner. And a little irritated— Mary's words still ringing in my ears. "Yes," I said. "I'd like to be part of the meeting. I'll see you in ten minutes."

"Great," Kira answered quickly. "See you soon." And then she hung up.

I sat for a moment, the phone still pressed to my ear, and wondered about my situation. Then I exhaled. Getting my life back was going to take some work. Starting now.

After putting my bowl in the kitchen sink, I got in my car and drove toward Kira's apartment complex. It was near the railroad, which I thought was kind of neat because she had a clear view of the train out her window. Even if it was a little loud sometimes.

When I knocked on her door, Kira's mother, Elise, answered. I tried not to cough as she blew out her cigarette smoke.

"Hi, Tessa," she said before turning around and walking back inside. Not exactly the warmest welcome.

"Hello." I tried to be extra cheerful when I was at Kira's

house. With its stale white walls and shaggy brown carpet, the place sometimes seemed a little lackluster. It just needed the right spirit to cheer it up.

"Thank goodness you're here," Kira called as she ran out from her bedroom. I was glad she was happy to see me. I had thought that maybe I was going to be an extra wheel.

"What's wrong?" I asked.

Her blonde curls were pulled into a messy half ponytail, and she fiddled with the bottom of her T-shirt. She sighed, and I looked past her to see her mother coughing over at the sink, where she was doing dishes. I was pleased to see that she'd put out her cigarette. I had tried to tell her once about the harmful effects of smoking, but she hadn't seemed worried.

"Izzie and Sam got into another fight," she whispered. "A bad one." She widened her eyes, and I felt my heart begin to race.

This was awful news! Izzie adored her college boyfriend. "Oh, no."

"And she got dropped from the soccer team."

My jaw dropped open. Poor Izzie! "She must be a mess."

"She is," Kira said, nodding. "It's like a tragic-a-thon. But all she cares about is Sam. She wants us to investigate him."

"An SOS investigation?"

Kira stepped back and then glanced down at the faded brown carpeting of her living room. "Well, yeah. I mean, if we're going to use it to uncover the copy-Kitten, why not use it to help our friend?"

"Because that's not what it's about," I said. "Kira, SOS was unethical and only caused us problems. That's why we stopped."

"Why *you* stopped," she corrected, and then met my eyes with a steady blue gaze. She looked over her shoulder toward her room and then back at me. "Okay," she said, trying to smile. "Right now we have enough drama anyway. Let's not talk about it in front of her. Deal?"

I nodded. It was not okay to spy on an ex-boyfriend and, in my opinion, not okay to spy at all. SOS was only restarting to catch the copy-Kitten.

"And besides," Kira added, undoing her half ponytail and resetting it. "Things are going to start looking up. You're going to totally fall in love with Chris! He's perfect for you."

I wanted to blow off the night, but that hardly seemed fair. Kira had finally found a boy that she liked and Izzie needed moral support. I wanted to be more involved. If this was the way to get back into the group, then fine.

Kira tsked, looking at me like I was the most injured soul on earth. "It's going to be okay, Tess," she said. "I know you've fallen off the popularity truck, and frankly, we've all been worried about you. But you're back now. And Chris Townsend is going to help you get there. You'll see."

I smiled, meeting her gaze. "You sound like Madame Corrine."

"The psychic?" Kira gasped. "She's the reason I hate fortune-tellers!"

Kira's mother turned off the sink and turned to us. "Oh, no," she said. "No more psychic hotlines in this house!"

"Mom," Kira interrupted. "I already said I was sorry!"

Her mother adjusted her robe and cursed under her breath as she walked across the apartment toward her room. I hated when Kira and her mother fought, which was surprisingly often. My mom never yelled at me, let alone threw things in my general direction when she was angry. Kira's household didn't follow the same rules.

I sighed. Kira was a great friend and a hardworking captain, but I wasn't sure I wanted her to be my matchmaker. Not after the dating debacle she got Izzie involved in this summer. Before she'd settled down with Sam, Izzie had let Kira set her up with a guy from her church. But honestly, Izzie shared part of the blame in the mess. She should have been able to recognize her own cousin!

"I'll go to the movie," I said, sighing. I had to do my part to reunite the Smitten Kittens. "But please understand that it's not a real date. I still want Aiden. This is just for the squad."

Kira clapped. "Yay! You're going to have a new boyfriend by the end of the night!"

My stomach turned at the thought. I just wanted my old boyfriend back, but each day that passed, I could feel it becoming more unlikely. At least my fake date could help me get something back: the Smitten Kittens.

As I sat on Kira's bed, listening to Izzie tearfully recount her fight with Sam, I glanced around Kira's room, at the mixture of music posters and cheer paraphernalia. The pictures of us stuck to the mirror of her vanity, a few folded so they cut Leona's face just enough to make her look like a Cyclops. And then there were the piles of clothes flowing from the closet. Kira had never been big into organization.

"Personally," Leona said, ignoring Izzie's sniffling, "I think you could do better than Sam. Have you seen that kid Franco in my Spanish class? He's *muy caliente*."

"Leona." Kira stomped her foot. "You know we don't speak Spanish, so don't try any secret codes." She twitched her mouth and then readjusted her stance. "Now which guy are you talking about?"

"But I like Sam," Izzie whined.

"I understand," I whispered. Izzie looked up, her green eyes brimming with tears. "And I'm sorry about the team too. But we'll get through this together," I said. "And I know that your boyfriend is number-one priority, but we also have to crack down on this copy-Kitten."

"Speaking of," Leona interrupted. "I haven't received the signed release form from you or Kira yet. Are you on board for Operation Knockoff?"

Kira and I turned to each other at the same time. It looked like we'd both been slacking. "I'll get it to you by lunch," I said to Leona. Kira pressed her lips in a smile and turned to Leona.

"I'll hand in mine right now."

I shifted a little uneasily but then tried to refocus as Kira began rummaging through the crumpled papers on her dresser.

"So," I began, looking between Izzie and Leona. "We'll do the movies tonight, but after the show, we'll plan the first SOS sting for tomorrow. Sound good?"

Izzie nodded, wiping at her nose with the back of her sleeve. Leona nodded approvingly. "Finally."

And with that, SOS was officially back and ready to investigate.

Something was off about all of us, but that would change soon. Once I was a bona fide member of the squad again, people would listen. Because overall, the skirt demanded respect. Even if I wasn't the captain anymore.

SOS
CHEATER REQUEST

CASE: 003
CLIENT: Izzie Edwards
SUBJECT: Samuel Facillo

Dear Ms. Edwards,

Thank you for your cheater request. Although we sympathize with your concerns that your college boyfriend is cheating, we regret that we cannot take on your case.

Because of your current status with the Smitten Kittens, you and your fellow cheerleaders are banned from our investigations. I'm sure you can understand the conflict.

We do hope that Mr. Facillo is in fact not cheating, but if you find out that he is, we trust you will do what's right and carry out the relationship termination on your own.

Thank you for thinking of us. And we offer you our sincerest wishes for your future.

Keep kicking ass,
SOS ☺
SOS
Text: 555-1863
Exposing Cheaters for Over Three Years

CHAPTER TWELVE

"YOU DID WHAT?" I DEMANDED, MY MOUTH HANG-
ing open as I stared at Izzie while she drove.

"I thought they could help," Izzie said, her face puffy from crying. She'd just admitted that she'd solicited help from the fake SOS in order to find out if Sam had been cheating on her!

"Izzie, why would you do that? Don't you remember what happened when I spied on Aiden?" If not, the small scar on my forehead should be a reminder.

"I know! It was stupid," she said, tears racing down her cheeks. "But what am I supposed to do? He said he wanted to take a break. Why would he need a break if there wasn't another girl involved?"

I shook my head. Okay, I knew the stats. And I knew it was not only possible, but probable that Sam had met someone else, but that didn't mean Izzie had the right to spy on him. "Don't take this the wrong way," I said softly, reaching out to touch her shoulder. "But Sam broke up with you. So technically, if he's seeing someone else, it's not cheating."

Izzie whipped her head toward me so fast, the car swerved. "You think he's seeing someone else?"

"Hey," I said, pointing at the windshield. "Watch the road." I was thankful to see the multiplex just ahead. "I'm not saying he is, but I just don't want you doing something crazy out of anger."

Izzie sniffled, resuming her gaze on the road as she turned into the movie-theater parking lot.

"That copy-Kitten can't be trusted, Izzie. You should know that. I promise we'll work through this. You just need to be patient."

Izzie nodded and parked her car before turning off the engine. "You're right," she said quietly. "Just because I'm desperate, it doesn't mean I can get in bed with the enemy. You know, like you did with Christian."

My face stung and I turned quickly to look out the passenger window. Even if Izzie didn't mean it as an insult, her words crushed me.

Izzie looked at me, her green eyes tired and sad. "I'm sorry that I didn't come to you first, Tess," she murmured. "But I needed a captain. I needed a leader."

I nodded in agreement. But after the obvious disarray of the squad, I wasn't sure if she was following the right captain anymore.

When we got inside, Kira hadn't arrived yet, but Leona was waiting in front of the concession stand, tapping one size-nine sneaker in annoyance. The bright neon lights across the ceiling flashed blue, green, and red across her glasses. Chris Townsend emerged from the line behind her with two Cokes. He smiled widely at me, and I swallowed hard. I was so not ready for this.

"Chris is so cute," Izzie whispered, her minty breath washing over the side of my face. "And you guys will look totally dreamy together."

I twitched my nose as I waved halfheartedly to Chris, watching as he and Leona made their way over to us. Chris's blond hair was perfectly messy, and his button-down shirt made his blue eyes stand out fantastically. And sure, he was cute enough—but he wasn't Aiden.

"Hey, Tessa," he said, pausing in front of me.

"Hello, Chris. You look nice." I tried to smile.

His face brightened. "Yeah? Well...um...you look nice too." He handed me one of the Cokes, then slid his now-empty hand in his pocket; then, as if rethinking it, he ran it through his hair instead.

"Nice shirt," Leona mumbled from next to me, adjusting her glasses as she looked over Chris, then turned away.

He glanced at her. "Oh. Thanks." Then he looked back to me. "So..." He let the word hang there, but I didn't know what to say! This date wasn't my idea. My fingers began to tremble, and I blinked quickly, chewing on my lip.

"I'm here!" Kira announced from behind us, and I turned to see her, walking up, waving her hands wildly. "Sorry I'm late." I immediately felt better. Waiting for Kira could have been an all-night affair.

As she passed behind Chris, she looked him over (pausing to get a good look at his rear), then gave me a big thumbs-up. I laughed.

Just then, the glass doors of the cinema swung open, and Joel came running in, skidding to a stop on the tile floor when he saw us all gathered in the lobby.

"And where were you?" Kira asked, just as he opened his mouth to talk. Joel's eyes flicked to mine, then back toward her.

"Sorry. My dad needed to put the car—"

"Whatev," she said, waving her hand. "I had to get a ride from my *mother* because you weren't answering your phone. I'm really unhappy." Kira pulled her glossy lips into a pout. I looked at Leona, who groaned next to me. This was awfully uncomfortable.

"Wow, Kira. You're so pleasant. No wonder he didn't answer the phone." Leona laughed, but Kira spun around so fast that it actually made us jump back a little.

"Shut your stupid mouth, Leona," she snapped. "And stay out of it."

My eyes widened. I'd never seen Kira lose it like this. It wasn't like Leona's harsh comments were something new.

"Whoa," Leona said, holding up her hands. "Back off, Dragon Lady. I was just being observant." When Kira seemed to calm down, Leona shrugged. "And besides, getting called stupid by *you* is almost like a compliment."

"Okay, okay," Joel said, stepping over to stand between my friends. "Keep it up, and you'll both be in time-out."

"Thanks, Dad," Leona said, walking away toward the movie entrance to check her phone.

I glanced over at Joel to find him grinning at me. His crooked smile made me sigh. I was glad to be here. Even if I was on a tragically misguided date, it was nice to be around friends.

"Do you want some popcorn?" Chris asked, his deep voice startling me as he touched my arm.

I glanced over at the concession stand. "Sure. No butter, though." Because those five pounds weren't going to lose themselves.

"What?" Joel asked, shaking his head. "You have to get butter on it." He paused, looking me over. "You're not one of those diet girls, are you?" He leaned in to whisper. "After all, I saw you inhale an entire pizza."

"Half!"

"And a Frappuccino."

Ooh…he had me there. I glanced at the group, glad Kira hadn't heard. Suddenly I felt like everyone was sizing me up. Literally.

"Tessa needs to get in shape before she comes back to the squad," Kira said, fluffing her curls and smoothing her lips together.

Joel scoffed as he pointed to me. "You're joking, right?" He glanced toward my…er…date. "Chris, do you believe that shit?"

"I think she looks great," Chris said, his hand grazing mine as he stood next to me. I gulped.

"Thanks." I tried to sound upbeat, but the idea of sitting in a darkened theater with Chris was making my stomach butterflies go from anxious to nauseous.

"Now get this girl some butter." Joel smiled at me. "And see if they have any gummy bears. I bet she likes gummy bears."

Hm. It just so happened that he was right.

"What about me?" Kira asked, her arms sliding around Joel's waist from behind. "Anything you want," he murmured over his shoulder to her, his voice low, sexy.

I felt queasy. I remembered when Aiden and I were like that. Oblivious to the people around us—just in love. I sniffled.

"Tessa." Leona called from across the lobby. She was standing with Izzie, who even from here looked like a complete wreck. "Let's go get seats. Now."

I glanced at Chris, who nodded.

"See you in there," Joel said with a smile before taking Kira's hand and walking toward the concessions.

We parked ourselves in the back row of the near-empty theater and tried to answer the movie trivia. After a few minutes, I took out my phone and called Aiden's dorm room, but all I got was his voice mail. I hung up.

"Stop calling him," Leona murmured from the seat next to me. "You're trying to look like you're on a date." She wasn't even looking in my direction, but I nodded anyway.

I heard loud giggling as the theater doors opened. I turned in my seat to see Kira being followed in by both Joel and Chris. She looked completely confident. The opposite of how I felt.

"She looks so pretty," I said.

"She always looks nice for Joel," Izzie replied.

As Kira made her way down the aisle, Leona got up and moved to the far corner by the wall (at least four seats away from Kira) and Izzie slid over next to her. Chris carefully balanced a tub of popcorn—with butter running down its side—as he sat next to me, and Kira dropped down on my other side. Joel paused before sinking down next to Kira.

"I've had the worst day," Kira said, turning to me as she fanned herself with her hand. "Mary has been calling me nonstop."

"Really?" My back flinched. "What about now?"

"You."

I widened my eyes. "I told her to back off," I said. "Remember, Kira, she isn't part of the squad anymore. You don't have to listen to her." Just thinking about Mary's betrayal was making my blood boil.

Kira reached over for a handful of popcorn. "I know," she said. "First she was rambling on about college, and honestly, Tess, you know how much I hate talking about the academic system. Mostly she wanted to hear your cheer status."

Seemed like I was the talk of the squad lately, only no one was talking *to* me. "And what about...other things?" I asked, not sure what Kira had updated her on regarding SOS. Just then I noticed how Joel was leaning forward, listening to our conversation. He was being a bit of a snoop. "We'll discuss this after the movie," I whispered to Kira, leaning back in my chair.

The lights dimmed as the movie started, and there was rustling as everyone got situated in their seats. I wasn't particularly excited to see this flick. I mean, I was always happy to watch attractive movie stars display their muscles in the name of action, but now it only made me think of Aiden. And that time when I stabbed him.

"I was wondering," Chris whispered, his breath reeking of Junior Mints. "Are you still coming to my party next weekend after this? I want you to."

There was a fluttering in my stomach. Sure, this movie could possibly already be considered a date, but now Chris was asking me on a second date. And although I was flattered, I was also scared senseless! I wasn't even sure that I liked Chris.

"Um..."

"We'll all be there, Chris," Leona said for me, leaning over in her seat to look down the aisle at us. "Thanks for asking."

"I have the perfect costume," Izzie cooed, clapping.

"Great," Chris said, glancing between us. Then he leaned back in his seat and placed his arm around me, kneading my shoulder with his fingers. I thought about moving, but I didn't want to be rude. Instead I picked up a handful of over-buttered popcorn and shoved it into my mouth.

"Oh." Kira jumped from next to me, startling me.

I looked over as she fished her cell phone out of her purse and glanced at the number. She bit her lip, bending forward in her seat. "It's Mary," she whispered.

"Do you want me to talk to her?" I asked. Because I had a few choice words for her.

Kira looked over her shoulder at me, as if surprised that I'd ask. "No. I'll handle it." She clicked the phone on and said, "Hold on," into the phone as she got up. "I'll be right back," she whispered to Joel, patting his leg as she stood up.

He nodded, still staring ahead, obviously riveted by the scene in the movie where the hero gets the girl. In bed.

"I have to go to the bathroom," Chris murmured, standing up. "I'll be right back?" I wasn't sure why he asked it as a question. Like I was going to say no?

"I'll come with," Leona called, getting up to scoot past me, following Kira and Chris down the movie aisle.

"Now?" I watched as the three left, illuminating the room with the hallway light. I heard a small squeak and looked over at Izzie. She was shifting uncomfortably in her seat like a five-year-old. "Seriously?" I asked.

"Uh- huh." I shook my head, pulling my legs up in the seat so that she could squeeze past me. Were they ditching me on purpose, or was it a coincidence that Izzie's and Leona's bladder filled at the exact moment that Mary Rudick called? Hm.

Once they were gone, I glanced over at Joel. He was sitting a seat away, biting his nails as he watched the movie, his legs spread out in front of him like he was lounging on a couch.

He looked sideways at me once and then did a double take. "Hey," he said, and smiled. It was a little dark, but I did notice the way his hazel eyes sparkled with the reflection of the movie screen.

Joel turned in the seat and crossed his legs, facing me. "Interesting company. Are your friends playing matchmaker?"

My smiled faded. "Yep. Awesome, right?"

"Not really."

I laughed. At least someone agreed with me.

"Chris's nice, though," he said, glancing at the screen as someone got shot. "A little bland if you ask me, but nice."

"I didn't ask," I responded.

"Very good, Crimson. I see you're working on your sarcasm."

I laughed and we both turned back to the movie, immersed in a long scene involving backward car chases and exploding gas stations. Eventually Joel exhaled loudly and I looked over at him.

"Man," he said, shifting in his seat and glancing at the door. "Did they forget about us or what?"

"Probably got sidetracked by the bright lights and candy boxes."

Joel looked at me, his mouth hanging open. He apparently hadn't expected that zinger, but he looked amused.

"Sorry." I shook my head. "I'm going overboard. I'm just not really feeling super-upbeat today."

"If it makes you feel better, despite this cool exterior, I'm suffering from some severe social anxiety disorder right now." He paused and then leaned over to whisper, "But I promise that if anyone asks, I'll tell them you were peppy beyond comprehension."

Aw. That was awful sweet of him. "Thanks."

"No problem." Joel rested the back of his head against the seat, watching me. "Oh," he said, holding up his finger. "Speaking of candy…"

Joel reached into his pocket and pulled out a box of gummy bears. "Just for you," he said, shaking the box temptingly before tearing into it.

"You've been keeping gummies in your pocket this whole time?" I asked.

He widened his eyes like it was a stupid question. "Of course."

I shook my head and turned back to the screen. After a second, he nudged my arm. "Here," he said, holding out the box. I put out my palm and he poured a few in. But then he paused and reached down to pinch some out. "Sorry," he said, popping them into his mouth before I could yank my hand away. "I get to keep all the red ones."

I giggled just as Kira appeared at the end of the aisle. "Hey!" She looked between Joel and me huddled together, fighting over the gummy bears.

Joel straightened in his seat and I shoved the handful of bears into my mouth, making my teeth stick together so I wouldn't have to talk. Besides, I might have been a little ticked at being cut out of the Smitten Kittens' loop. Again.

When Kira got down the aisle and sat next to me, she lowered her head in my direction. "Izzie's having a mini-meltdown in the bathroom," she whispered.

"What?" I mumbled through a mouth full of bears.

"It's okay; Leona's there." She looked down the aisle. "Where's Chris?"

"Bathroom." Actually it'd been a while, but I didn't want to really consider it.

Kira crinkled her nose, then took the box of gummy bears out of Joel's hand and poured a bunch into her hand. "It's fine," she said to me between bears. "You can ride with me—and after I drop Joel off, we'll set up the...you know."

She was so covert.

I nodded, wondering what had gone on outside the movie doors. All I knew was that Kira was here and Izzie was crying in the bathroom being comforted by Leona, of all people.

Just then the door opened and Chris came in, holding a package of gummy bears and beaming at me. I heard Joel snicker from down the aisle. As Chris sat down, he offered them to me.

"Want some?" he asked.

I turned and smiled politely at him. "No, thanks. I'm full." I felt Kira look at me, but by the time I glanced over, she was snuggled next to Joel with her head on his shoulder.

There was a small pang in my back, but I thought it away and tried to focus on the movie. I was tired of being insignificant. I wanted some power back. Or at least, whatever power I was willing to take.

(CODE PINK) SOS
INTER-KITTEN COMMUNICATION

Dear Smitten Kittens,

This is a reminder that we are on high alert. You should not, in any way, try to contact the copy-Kitten without SOS approval. Even for emotional support.

Any Kitten found to be consorting with the enemy will face suspension.

If you have any questions, please use the Code Pink hotline at 555-0101. Do NOT make any communications on the SOS database or e-mail lines.

Keep smiling,

Leona ☺

CHAPTER THIRTEEN

THE NEXT NIGHT THE SMITTEN KITTENS AND I were parked in the back lot of the school, working on a lead. The evening was getting dark, but the moon was full, giving us just enough light to see without night vision.

"Pass the Cheez Doodles," Leona called to me from the backseat.

"Watch the upholstery," Kira snapped at her as I passed along the bag. Kira had finally gotten her first car this summer after her mom won a disability settlement with the state. She was stoked.

Izzie sniffled from the backseat. My eyes weakened as I looked back at her. Since the movies, she'd been inconsolable. Apparently while we were there, Sam had returned all of her stuff to her grandparents' house, including the mixed CD she'd made him. Worse than that, he wouldn't take her calls or e-mails. "Hey," I said. "You hanging in there?"

"I guess," she murmured, staring out the back window. Poor thing hadn't even had the strength to fix her hair today. It hung lifelessly under her black cap.

I glanced at Leona as she crunched on a Cheez Doodle, looking very sympathetic. "It's going to be fine," she said, reaching over the crackly bag to offer some snacks to Izzie. "Sam's not seeing anyone else. He just needed a break." Leona darted her eyes to mine, and I knew she didn't believe it either.

"Pom-poms up," Kira said, ducking down in the front seat. We all did the same, which was followed by a series of little patters—the sound of Cheez Doodles dumping on the floor mats. Kira growled next to me.

Leona had intercepted a Knockoff communication of a cheater request against Calvin Murdock. We'd been following him all night, including here, at his football practice. Until now, there had been no sign of a copy-Kitten. Obviously she was in over her head.

I peeked over the dash to see a girl walking in the distance, laughing and talking into her phone. I bent down and grabbed a pair of binoculars, then straightened and focused in on her face.

"No way," I whispered.

"Who is it?" Kira said, looking sideways at me from behind her steering wheel. I dropped the binoculars and stared at her.

"It's Chloe Ferril." My heart was racing.

"Ew, so not in the mood to deal with her negativity," Kira said, scrunching her nose.

"Told you," Leona said, licking the orange cheese off her fingers.

"She's not the copy-Kitten." Kira snorted, glancing into the backseat.

"No? Then what is she doing here? Looking for the skank convention? Because I'm pretty sure they hold that over at your house."

Kira snarled and reached back, as if to grab Leona's black tank, but I held her back. "Ladies!" I whisper-yelled. "This is not the time, and it's certainly not the place!" The escalation of in-squad violence was alarming. They definitely needed my leadership.

Izzie started crying into her hands and we all turned to look at her. "I hate when you guys fight," she mumbled. "It makes me think of Sam."

Leona rolled her eyes and leaned back into the seat and patted Izzie's leg. "I'm sorry, Iz," she said. "We're done."

We were quiet for a few minutes, staring out the windshield until the sound of Leona's crunching began to fill the car again. Kira looked sideways at me.

"Is Leona right?" she whispered. "Do you really think Chloe's the copy-Kitten?"

"Hm…" I took out the camera with the extra-zoom lens and pushed in to focus. Chloe (not surprisingly) was dressed in a black, cleavage-busting goth dress with tons of makeup. She was still talking on her phone and—actually—stumbling like she might be intoxicated.

"Don't think so," I said. "She looks drunk."

Just then Chloe rolled her ankle and fell onto a parked car, laughing as she pushed off the hood and looked around, pointing her finger at someone in the driver's seat of the car.

"Classy," Leona said from the backseat, sitting up.

"Can we just go?" Izzie asked in a low voice. "I want to drive by Sam's. Kira, you promised on the way home we would."

I shot a glance at Kira. She shouldn't be condoning this sort of behavior.

"Tessa," Leona called from the back. "Can you please get a handle on this? Kira is a worse influence on Izzie than…well, me."

Kira gave Leona a dirty look in the rearview mirror, then she glared at me. "Don't start, Tessa," she said. "I've been busting my tail trying to weather this flood."

"It's storm."

"Yeah," Kira replied. "A shit storm."

I stared back at her; her blonde hair (although still shiny) was starting to look worn. Her normally well-lined eyes looked naked from neglect. She was right. She had been working hard.

"I'm sorry," I said. "I should have been here for you sooner."

At this, the tight lines around Kira's mouth loosened, and she smiled. "I'm just glad you're here now. And I can't wait until you're back on the squad. I want things to go back to normal."

"This is sweet and all," Leona said, leaning up between the seats and pointing out the windshield. "But we just missed something big."

Both Kira and I turned to follow Leona's chewed-off fingernail, which pointed toward the parked car. Just then the driver got out. She was talking to Chloe, and when I lifted my camera, I gasped when I saw her.

"Chicken of the Sea," I murmured.

"Who is it?" Kira demanded, yanking the camera away from my face.

"It's Mary." I looked back at Leona.

Leona shook her head, twisting her face. "What the frig is she doing here? Last night she told us she was giving up on her anti-Tessa campaign and going back to Washington State."

"No," I said. "That's where Aiden goes to school. Mary goes to college in California."

"Not anymore," Kira said offhandedly. "She transferred to Washington at the beginning of the year." She lowered the camera and looked at me. "She didn't tell you?"

"What? No. When did she—"

"Hey," Izzie said, motioning toward the parking lot. "What kind of car does Aiden drive?"

"Jetta," I answered, still staring at Kira.

"Oh." Izzie clapped, sounding excited. "Then he's here!"

I snapped my head toward the parking lot. And I saw it. It was definitely Aiden's white Jetta passing by us. It slowed to a stop, just as Mary looked toward it and waved.

She said something to Christian's sister and turned on her dark heels. I picked up the binoculars to watch. Her thick brown hair bounced off her shoulders, and her red dress fit her athletic frame perfectly. She crossed to Aiden's car and leaned in the passenger window, talking to him. She laughed, glancing around the parking lot once. And then she got in.

"Did she just…" But Kira didn't finish, because just then, they started driving away. From the back window, I saw her lean over.

And kiss him.

"It could be a tragic misunderstanding like the last time," Kira said quietly as we drove the darkened streets of Redmond. "If there's one thing we know about Aiden, it's not to jump to conclusions."

I nodded. My stomach was sick, but like I'd told Izzie, if you're broken up, it doesn't count as cheating. It just counts as sucky.

"Well, makes sense why she's been trying to keep you off the squad. She obviously hates you."

I gasped and put my cool hand over my forehead. This couldn't be happening. Betraying me on a cheer level was completely different than betraying me on a boyfriend level. I mean, Mary started SOS! She should have better morals. "I wonder if they're dating," I murmured. "What if she's his girlfriend?" The thought made me sick.

"I can see why she didn't tell you she switched schools. Makes you wonder how many times they've met up at college," Leona commented from the back.

I spun around to face her, and her eyes widened behind her glasses.

"Um...which I'm sure was never."

Good gravy. This was the new worst night of my life. My heart felt completely trampled, doused, and lit on fire. I rubbed my eyes with my thumbs. I'd need to see the hairdresser tomorrow. And the manicurist, the aromatherapist, and, lastly, the barista at Starbucks. Oh, yes. It would be a full-day self-help extravaganza.

There was a sniffle from the back (Izzie) and it struck me: I wasn't the only Kitten with a broken heart. It was selfish of me to think of myself at a time like this, when we were on a mission. No, if anything, we'd just found the perfect suspect. "Stop the car, K," I said. "We have to get back to the assignment."

Kira looked over at me, impressed. "Really?"

"Yes. I let us down once, but I refuse to do it again. Aiden has obviously moved on, and maybe it's time that I do too." I was trying to sound brave, but my own words were making my chest ache. "Listen, right now the Smitten Kittens are in disarray. I've lost Aiden, Izzie's lost Sam. Leona—"

She coughed from the back, letting me know that the Marco story was still top secret.

I nodded, flashing her an apologetic glance. "The point is, we all have problems, and to solve them is going to take true commitment. But with a copy-Kitten out there trashing our name and meddling in our lives, we'll never get the focus we need." I stared at the girls, trying to see if they were all on board. Izzie and Leona smiled at me encouragingly while Kira stared out the windshield, continuing to drive.

"It's time the squad unites," I said. "I'll date Chris—do whatever you want. But I want back on the squad. And Kira, you're the captain. You can overrule any vote." I straightened my back as Kira's mouth opened; she looked a little surprised.

"I don't know," she said. "I'm not sure you're ready for it, Tess."

I reset my jaw. "Are you saying that *you* won't let me on the squad?"

"Of course she's not saying that," Leona announced from the back. "We need your leadership, Tess."

"Excuse me," Kira said, looking at her in the mirror. "I'm the captain, and I make the decisions."

I considered telling Kira about my conversation with Principal Pelli, but no matter how unreasonable she was being, I couldn't hurt her like that. She wanted to be captain so badly.

"Think about it," I said, turning to Kira. "For now, take me home. I need to devise a new plan. I have a main suspect, and I know she's going to slip up." (Being around Aiden sometimes caused lapses in judgment.) "And when she does, I want to be the one busting her!" Because this mission had just become very personal.

Leona laughed. "You're going all badass on us, Tess."

"It's *BA*. And I haven't even begun to catfight," I said seriously.

"Well," Izzie began, "is it Chloe or Mary?"

I narrowed my eyes, replaying the night in the bookstore when Chloe touched Aiden and then the horrific scene of Mary kissing him. Then I closed my eyes. "I don't know. But I'll find out." Then turned to Kira. "Now drive."

Kira gritted her teeth and shook her head. "Whatever you say, Tessa."

I watched her, unsure where the animosity was coming from, because if there was one thing I knew, it was that Smitten Kittens didn't hold animosity toward each other.

But then again, maybe she didn't consider me a Smitten Kitten anymore.

When I got home, my mother was in the kitchen, sitting at the table clipping coupons out of a magazine. She looked surprised to see me when I walked in. It might have been my head-to-toe black spy wear.

"Hey, honey," she said suspiciously. "Where are you coming from?"

I sighed and dropped my keys on the granite of the kitchen counter with a clank before sitting down next to her at the table. "I've had a bad night," I said.

"Oh, no. How bad?"

I looked up to see my mother's eyes wide with concern. Her graying hair was pulled tight in a low bun at the nape of her neck.

"Mom," I said, feeling my lower lip begin to quiver. "Aiden's dating another girl." And with that, I promptly fell apart.

"Shh…" my mother soothed, reaching over to brush back my hair as I laid my head on the cloth of the kitchen table. "Are you sure?"

"I saw him with her tonight," I said, my voice choked off from the tears. "I saw them kiss."

My mother tsked, and I felt her rest her cheek on mine. "It'll be okay, sweetie."

"It won't," I said. "He was with Mary Rudick."

"Your ex-captain?" My mother straightened up and took me by the chin, helping me do the same. "But that's against Smitten Kitten rules!" Her normally pale skin had grown a little pink in the cheeks.

I nodded. "I know. My own cheermate betrayed me. She's even been telling the squad not to let me rejoin."

"She can't do that!"

I started tearing up again. Right then, I couldn't even be angry; I was just so hurt by Aiden. "I love him, Mom. And he doesn't love me anymore."

My mother shook her head. "I'm sure that's not true, Tessa." She gave me a reassuring smile. "You're a wonderful, beautiful girl. Aiden's in college. Maybe he needs some time. Maybe he needs to figure out some things about himself right now."

I sniffled, trying to decide if my mother was just trying to make me feel better or if she really thought Aiden still loved me. "I'm going to a party," I said weakly. "The squad wants me to give Chris Townsend a chance."

My mother smiled. "He's a very nice boy. Cute, too."

I laughed. "Yeah."

My mother reached out, putting her hand over mine on the table. "Why don't you give it a try? Honey, if you and Aiden are right for each other, he'll come back. And if not..." She furrowed her brow and didn't finish her sentence. But that was okay; I didn't really want her to.

"I'll try," I said, twitching my nose. "Thanks, Mom." I leaned over to give her a hug, holding back my tears. I was glad she was here tonight to comfort me. I knew the Smitten Kittens couldn't do it right now, with all the mess we were in. And with Izzie's trouble, I hardly felt right asking.

"It's going to be okay," my mother whispered in my ear as she held me.

I closed my eyes, leaning into her shoulder. Right now, I *really* needed to hear that.

ASSIGNMENT 1

7:00 A.M., SEPTEMBER 19

The operative waited patiently behind the blue Waste Management Dumpster. It smelled like rotten banana peels and sweat socks over there, but it was the best place from which to view the high school's music room. Riley played bass in the band, and the operative had discovered that he and Megan had begun meeting there before school to talk. Or maybe more.

As a figure walked into the classroom, the operative crouched down, her black boots squishing in the sludge that was leaking from under the Dumpster. She crinkled her nose and took out her video camera to begin recording.

It was Riley. His navy blue T-shirt looked wrinkled, and she was almost positive that it didn't match the track pants he was wearing. She wondered about the sudden change in his appearance.

Megan appeared. She came running in the room, her straight hair trailing behind her like a blonde ribbon.

From outside, the operative couldn't hear what they were saying, and she hadn't had enough time to plant a recorder. No. She'd have to use her lip-reading ability again. She was proud of the progress, really. Those online courses were very thorough.

Megan was talking, her arms flailing around her as she did.

She looked upset. The operative narrowed her eyes and readjusted her feet in the sludge. She moved her lips along with Megan's.

"Riley, it's over. I don't care. Jenn is going to find out! Yes— you know I do! Look, with this rumor about SOS going around, I can't risk it!"

Right then, Megan's lips began to tremble, making it hard for the operative to translate her words. Instead she pondered her next move.

If Megan cut off the relationship, Jenn would never find out about the *almost* affair with her best friend and boyfriend. That wouldn't do.

The operative stood, her blood pumping as she walked closer to the window, not even trying to stay hidden anymore. But the subjects weren't looking at her; they were staring at each other, looking heartbroken.

"Aw…" the operative muttered bitterly. "Maybe next time you don't mess with an attached guy." Once at the window, the operative leaned against it, running her fingers quietly down the glass as she recorded them.

Riley reached over, taking Megan's hands as she cried, looking at the floor. He was murmuring something, something that looked like "I love you."

Megan tilted her head toward Riley—her mascara smudged under her eyes, causing her makeup to become a monster-movie disaster. She said something, but the operative couldn't read it. But she could guess.

Then it happened. Megan got up on her tiptoes, and Riley put his hands on her cheeks and leaned down, touching his lips to hers. Slowly they became more passionate until it was a full-on make out. The operative smiled and clicked off her camera.

Bingo. With that, she pulled a business card out of her black wraparound trench coat. She turned the stiff paper over in her hand. Then she brought the card to her mouth and kissed it, leaving a smooth, dark print.

Pulling back, she smiled. Then she took the card and slapped it—lipstick side first—against the window with a loud bang so it stuck there. Both Riley and Megan jumped apart, but the operative turned, flipping her black hood over her hair, and began walking across the parking lot. Away from them. Away from the smell of trash.

She could hear the window open behind her, probably to pull in the card. And even from a few yards away, she heard Megan gasp.

Now that Megan and Riley knew they were being followed, things would change. But first, there was time for revenge.

CHAPTER FOURTEEN

I'D JUST CAUGHT MY FAVORITE GUY WITH MY NOT- so-favorite ex-captain, and I couldn't even enjoy the weekend. I spent it on the couch with a pint of Chubby Hubby ice cream and a *CSI* marathon—at least some of those people were worse off than me. To make life more tragic, I had to go to school on Monday looking halfway decent. The whole "getting back on the squad" image.

I'd just arrived when I saw Joel leaning against my locker, dressed in dark jeans and a white Nirvana T-shirt, with perfectly mussed hair. Everything about him looked comforting—maybe because I felt like a perfect disaster.

"Oh, man," he said, pushing off the metal locker to walk toward me, taking my backpack off my shoulder. "Kira said you were upset, but damn, Tess. You look *bad*!"

I smiled. "Thanks, Joel. That really helps."

He stepped back, looking proud. "You're getting more and more sarcastic every day. I'm loving it."

"Glad somebody is." I walked over to my locker, swirling the combo and looking over my shoulder at Joel. "I'm sorry," I said with a sigh, and opened the locker to grab my language arts materials. "I have a lot going on, including faking perky. It's so unpleasant." When I found my notebook, I took my backpack from Joel's hands and set it on the floor of the hallway. I unzipped it and tucked my book in. When I was done, I turned around to Joel and slammed my locker shut.

"Now," he said, putting his hands in his pockets. "How are you *really*?" He pressed his lips together in sympathy, but I wished he would smile. It made me feel better.

"How much has Kira told you?"

"Up to the kiss between the ex-captain chick and your ex-boyfriend."

I closed my eyes and scrunched my nose, the sight coming back to me all too quickly. "Thanks for reminding me."

"Sorry." He moved a little closer to me, filling me with the smell of him. Shampoo, soap, light cologne. "She said you took it like a champ and even asked for her to get you on the squad without a vote. Pretty bold."

I nodded. "That's true. I think it's time for all the Smitten Kittens to get their lives in order." I certainly couldn't tell him about the copy-Kitten, but I was sure he already knew about Izzie and Sam.

Joel licked his lips, watching the ground as he seemed to think this over. "Brave answer, Tessa. Now again, how do you *really* feel?"

I blinked quickly, my stomach beginning to twist with the pressure of thinking about it. "Peachy." But when I looked up to meet Joel's eyes, my vision began to blur. By Cleopatra's crown! I was starting to cry.

"Tessa?" someone called, and I sniffled quickly and looked down the hall. It was Megan Wright. She was jogging down the hall toward me, her books in her hand. "Could you do me a favor?" she asked, looking back over her shoulder down the hallway. "Will you tell Ms. Lipton that I'm sick or something?" She looked panicked as she continued to glance around, smiling politely at Joel once.

"Is everything all right?" I asked, my heart rate accelerating. "Do you need help?"

Megan swallowed hard, and for a minute, I thought she was going to tell me what was wrong; instead she shook her head. "I just have to get out of here," she whispered. "You'll tell Ms. Lipton, though?"

I nodded, feeling truly worried.

"Thanks, Tessa." She exhaled before turning around. "Oh," she said, looking back at me. "I heard you're thinking of getting back on the Smitten Kittens."

"Yep."

"I'm glad. They need you." Then she turned and hurried down the hall, her sandals flopping on the linoleum floor as she ran toward the exit.

"What was that about?" Joel asked, bumping his shoulder into mine.

I sighed. "I have no idea. But whatever it is, it's not good." I looked over, startled by just how close his face was to mine. Honeycombs! He was very handsome up close.

"Definitely not," he said, quietly, his eyes flickering to my mouth. We stood, somewhat frozen, until the tardy bell rang. It snapped me awake.

"Dang it," I said, spinning toward the English hallway. "I'm late!"

Joel was looking down at the ground, his eyebrows pulled together, as if he was in deep thought. I wasn't sure why he looked so confused, but I did know that I wanted to avoid detention.

"I have to run," I said, ducking down to catch his eyes. "I'll see you later?"

He straightened up, staring at me with a curious look on his face. "Um...sure. Yeah, I'll catch you later, Tess."

I curled my lip at him, not sure why he'd suddenly gotten so weird. When I gave him a wave and turned to jog down the hall to class, I thought I might have heard him call my name, but when I glanced back, he was gone.

I was pretty sure I scored less than an A on that language arts test I'd taken about *Death of a Salesman*. Ms. Lipton kept calling on me, then having other students correct my wrong answers. It was humiliating. And I felt like a science experiment during lunch because everyone was staring at me. Apparently Chloe had caught sight of Aiden and Mary too, but she wasn't as restrained as I was. She told the entire school. And although they asked politely (which I appreciated), the theme of today's interactions was, "How is Tessa handling it?"

When the day was over, I was completely relieved, not to mention a little overwhelmed with emotion. But I was determined to make it home before even one tear eked out.

When I got outside, I noticed that the Washington sky had imploded! It was cloaked in dark gray rain clouds. Ick. It was dreadful.

Feeling the first sprinkle touch my nose, I glanced up once more before dashing toward my car. I jogged across the parking lot and unlocked my door, happy that I'd just beaten the storm, as the rain began to hit my window in fat splatters.

I refused to think about how perfectly this rain complemented my crumbling life. I stuck my key in the ignition and turned it. There was a series of clicks, but otherwise nothing happened. "Oh, no," I said, trying it again. Nada.

I slapped my hand across the steering wheel, feeling annoyed. Even my car was breaking up with me? I stared at it, anger welling up in me, thinking about Mary. About Kira. About...Aiden. I slapped my steering wheel again, feeling it sting my hand.

"Stupid car," I mumbled. I hit it again. "Stupid, stupid, stupid..." I left my key dangling in the ignition as I beat the leather steering wheel with my fists, screaming louder with each hit.

There was a knock at my window and I jumped, out of breath and shaking. Joel was out there with his backpack over his head, trying to block the rain. Embarrassed and still a bit crazed, I opened the door.

"You're beating up your car," he said, as if it was just a casual observation.

I nodded, not sure I could respond. My throat was still sore from yelling.

"Do you need a ride?" he asked loudly as the rain began to pour around him.

"Yeah," I answered. "I think my battery's dead." I grabbed my bag off the seat and moved to get out, where I was immediately pelted with water.

"I don't have jumper cables," he shouted over the sound of the rain, reaching out to hold his backpack over my head as we walked toward his car. It didn't help keep me dry, but I thought it was an awfully sweet gesture anyway.

"My dad has some in my garage," I offered. I wasn't sure when my parents would be home, so I'd need to find someone to get my car started again.

"Great," Joel said, putting his hand on my back to lead me forward. "Let's go get them."

I sat in Joel's front seat, my wet hair sticking to my forehead. I looked sideways at him and he laughed, pointing at me. I felt my mouth form into a pout as I flipped down the vanity mirror and tried to unstick my hair.

"Sorry," he said, holding up his hands in apology. "I don't mean to laugh. I'm just not used to seeing you looking so...wet."

We both shifted with the uncomfortable connotation of his word choice.

"I mean damp," he said quickly, then furrowed his brow. "Rained on?"

"Rained on works." I wasn't clear how Joel and I were supposed to act around each other because I'd never had a good guy friend before—other than Aiden—and I was pretty sure that didn't count.

"I'll just take you home now," he mumbled, starting his car.

We drove to my house, easing into a conversation about school (who knew *Death of a Salesman* was totally heartbreaking!) and, oddly enough, cheerleading. When Joel pulled into my driveway, it was still pouring. I hated the idea of making him jump my car when the weather was so abysmal.

"Actually," I said, tilting my head to look at him. "You don't have to take me back to my car. The weather stinks. I'll ask my parents when they get home tonight. It should clear up by then."

"Really? I don't mind," Joel said, reaching to turn off his ignition.

"Thanks anyway. I'm just going to go in and watch TV until my parents get here." But dread slipped over me as I looked back at my house. I didn't want to be alone. It left too much time to...think. Not to mention that there was still a copy-Kitten out there with a habit of breaking in my house. And depending on who it was, I wasn't sure how violent they'd be. I bit my lip, daring myself to go in.

"Everything okay?" Joel asked. I watched him, gauging the concern in his expression.

"Do…do you want to come in?" I asked quickly. "I can make you a sandwich or something."

Joel looked at my house and then back at me, seemingly conflicted. "Uh…sure. But I'm not all that hungry."

My stomach stopped doing flips and I exhaled. I was so glad I wouldn't have to be alone. After the last few days, my nerves were shot.

Joel and I both got out, and he trailed me as we approached my front door. Just then, the rain stopped. Joel and I looked at the sky at the same time.

"Figures, right?" he asked with a laugh.

We walked inside my house, and I dropped my useless car keys on the counter, grabbing the house phone as I went. I'd have to call my father and leave him a message so that he'd know my car needed a jump. But before I could dial, it rang in my hands.

I shot a glance at Joel, hoping he wouldn't think I was a bad host for answering while I had company. Oh, no. What if it was Aiden? I hadn't talked to him since I'd seen him with Mary. What would I say?

"You going to get that?" Joel asked, pointing to the phone in my hand.

I nodded absently, looking down at it. Resting my hand on the cool granite counter, I took a steadying breath before returning the phone to my ear. "Hello?"

"Tess?" It was Kira. I exhaled.

"Thank goodness it's you. I was afraid it was…" I stopped. It wasn't Aiden. He wasn't even trying to call me.

"Afraid it was what?" Kira asked, sounding distracted.

"Never mind. What's up, K? I just got home from school, and I nearly collapsed from the horribleness of it."

"Ugh," she said. "I know. I heard everyone whispering about you." She snapped her gum loudly and then continued. "I meant to tell you, Leona had a run-in with Chloe. All but accused her of being the copy-Kitten. But I guess Chloe shoulder-bumped her and stormed out. Now Leona thinks she's totally guilty."

Shoulder-bumping was hardly new for Chloe, but that was an interesting development. Still, I had company. "Um…I don't know. We'll definitely have to…look into it." I was having trouble talking on my end with an audience. I glanced over to see Joel walking toward my living room wall, looking at all of our family pictures hanging there. Including several of Aiden and me.

"Cute," he whispered, pointing to a picture of me in a pink dance costume with missing teeth and pigtails.

I smiled at him before turning away, pressing the phone to my ear. "Can I call you back in a little bit?" I asked Kira, lowering my voice.

"Sure." She sighed. "I'm waiting for Joel to come over anyway. I don't know where he is. Have you seen him?" She sounded hopeful.

"Um…" Should I tell her he was here? I thought that maybe I should, but then I wondered if it would cause friction. I'd just asked her to get me on the squad; I didn't want to jeopardize that with a misunderstanding. I decided it was best to just ask Joel to leave. "I haven't," I said, feeling bad about lying. "But stop worrying. He's totally smitten. Promise." Although I was pretty positive that Joel was head over heels for Kira, we hadn't exactly talked about his feelings for her today.

She squealed. "He so is, right?"

"Absolutely."

"Thanks, Tess. I think I was just having a low-self-esteem moment. You always know how to cheer me up."

"Talk to you soon," I said, feeling horrible. I knew that I hadn't done anything wrong by inviting Joel in, but it was inappropriate. It had to be.

I breathed in through my nose and straightened my posture. Then I spun around and smiled at Joel.

"Second grade," I said, motioning toward the pink-costumed picture.

"Pretty cute, tiny Crimson."

I laughed. "Thanks." I was about to ask him to leave but then decided that it wouldn't be awful to let him stay a few more minutes. It might be selfish, but I really wanted the company. "Would you like a glass of lemonade?" I asked.

"Please." Joel put his hands in his pockets and made his way over to my couch.

I poured us each a glass of lemonade and carried them over to him, taking the seat across the room from him in the lounger. "So," I said. "Are you going to Chris's party next weekend?"

Joel lifted an eyebrow. "I might. You?"

I sipped at my drink and then set it on the coaster on the side table. "Yeah, I guess. Part of my deal with the squad is that I need to date someone…more appropriate. They think Chris is the one."

Joel's mouth opened, and he set his glass down and leaned forward, resting his elbows on his knees to stare at me. "Are you serious? They're forcing you to go out with him...what? Because he's a jock?"

"No." I shook my head. "Nobody's forcing me. They just think it'd be a good idea. I don't know."

"Do you like him?"

"I...I don't really know him."

"You don't like him."

My heart began to beat a little faster, and I sat up straighter. "Chris Townsend is a perfectly nice guy. He plays football, gets good grades. What's not to like?"

Joel smiled. "Um...everything you just mentioned."

I shook my head. "Don't be judgmental. Chris is great."

Joel pursed his lips and then leaned forward to pick up his glass and slowly sipped from it. "Not saying he's not. Just wondering if he's great for you."

I watched as Joel drank from his glass until it was gone, then he stood up and glanced around the room one more time. "I should probably take off," he said. "I'm supposed to go meet up with Kira."

Despite the small twinge in my back, I stood up to walk him to the door. "Thanks for the ride," I said, taking his glass as we got to the kitchen.

Joel paused, standing directly in front of me and looking down. "Anytime." He smiled, his signature crooked grin, then moved to the door to let himself out.

"I'll see you around, tiny Crimson."

I watched as he walked out, but the minute he was gone, I turned the dead bolt and went straight to my room. As I lay there on my bed, I reminded myself of all the reasons I should focus on Chris. And how he was...perfect.

SOS
CHEATER REQUEST

CASE: 004
CLIENT: Nancy Dwire
SUBJECT: Michael Machovelli

We have received your cheater request and are delighted to inform you that your assignment has been scheduled. This notice is to let you know that the process will begin shortly.

Mr. Machovelli is accused of having a sexual relationship with an unnamed accomplice, dating all the way back to June.

SOS will inform you of our findings as soon as possible.

Keep kicking ass,
SOS ☺
SOS
www.thecheaterreports.blogspot.com
Text: 555-1863
Exposing Cheaters for Over Three Years

CHAPTER FIFTEEN

NOT A WORD FROM AIDEN. I HADN'T TRIED TO CALL
him, and even though it crushed me not to hear from him, I didn't
know what I'd do if he called anyway. Instead I tried to focus on
the squad—getting the cheers together in my head (although I
wasn't technically a Smitten Kitten yet) and keeping my eyes out
for signs of the copy-Kitten.

But at home, it felt like the old days, the days when I was lost
and confused. Lonely.

My cell vibrated in the pocket of my jeans, and I wiggled it out
as I made my way to the couch in the living room. I glanced at the
caller ID and my heart skipped a beat. Huckleberry Finn! It was
Aiden's dorm room number.

My fingers trembled as they held the phone. "Hello?" I asked
quietly.

"Tess, I have to talk to you. I'm so sorry—"

I held the phone away from my ear as I took a moment to
breathe. I wouldn't be able to handle what came next. Not able to
hear that he'd moved on—to Mary!

I gripped the pink connection to Aiden, at the call I'd been
hoping would come for two days. And then I hung up. I closed
my eyes. Someone at school must have told Aiden that there
were rumors about him and Mary. And since I hadn't called him

(which I had been prone to do), he would have figured out that I knew.

Feeling shaky, I lay across the couch, staring at the blank TV. If only I could just start over, start fresh somewhere else. But I knew that wouldn't really solve my issues. I needed to stop dwelling and get my ribbon on straight.

After a minute of dwelling, I grabbed my phone and scrolled through my speed dial. When I found Leona's number, I exhaled.

"Hey, Tessa," Leona said when she answered. Her voice sounded choked off, sad. Hearing that made my fur stand on end.

"What's wrong?" I asked, sitting up on the couch. It wasn't like Leona to sound so vulnerable. Heck, I was calling her for strength.

"There's been an incident," she said with a sniffle.

I gasped and covered my mouth with my hand. "Is everyone okay?"

"Everyone but me."

"Oh, no." Grief flooded me. "Is this about Marco?" Leona had been accessorizing again. I thought it'd meant that Marco had decided to accept her as she was, but apparently things hadn't gone according to her plan.

"No, my cat ran away. Of course it's about Marco!" she choked out between sobs.

My shoulders slumped. "Hey," I said soothingly. "Why don't you come over and we'll have a beauty-treatment night?" Some self-therapy could be just what the beautician ordered right now.

"Yeah, sounds like a blast."

"I have pore minimizer...."

"Fine," Leona said, unable to turn down an offer that would help her complexion. "I'll be there in ten minutes. And I'll bring the cucumbers."

* * *

When Leona arrived, I was shocked. Her dark eyes were ringed in red, her nose was pink and stuffy, and her hair—well, it was just too awful to describe.

We started in the kitchen, slicing up cucumbers for our eyes and mixing oatmeal and egg for our faces. Once our products set, we moved into my bedroom, surrounded by soft colors and fluffy comforters.

"Okay," I said as I smeared a lumpy spoonful on her face. "Tell me what happened."

Leona sighed, staring up at the ceiling as I smoothed the mixture under her eyes. "Marco told me that he's not interested. Turns out...he has a girlfriend."

I nearly dropped the bowl of goop into my lap. "What? Are you serious?"

"Deadly. He's been seeing some chick from West Washington since summer but never brought it up. So when I took your advice and asked him to ask me out..." Her eyes welled up. "He said he couldn't."

"Oh, Leona!" I set down the mixture and wrapped my arms around her in a hug. This was horrible! She'd been trying so hard. I saw her in the halls when she was talking to Marco, and she was smiling! She smiled for him!

I straightened up and held her by the shoulders, giving her my very best supportive expression. "This isn't awful," I said. "At least you found out that he had a girlfriend. This could have gone on until senior prom."

Leona pressed her lips together, blinking away her tears. "You're right," she said. "And at least he wasn't trying to cheat on his girlfriend."

"Exactly." Her eyes locked on mine, and I knew we were both thinking the same thing. "Sam?" I asked.

"I think he was seeing someone else before he broke it off with Izzie," Leona said quietly. "And I have to tell you, Tess, I think Izzie has gone off the deep end. She isn't answering calls, and when I went by her house last night, her car was gone. I think she might be stalking him."

It was entirely possible that Izzie was stalking. She was very dedicated by nature. I clenched my jaw, trying to think of the right course of action. "This is bad," I murmured.

"Horribly bad."

Just then my cell phone vibrated on my rosewood side table. "It's Kira," I said to Leona.

"Power trip," she sang out, picking up the bowl of oatmeal and walking over to my vanity to continue the application process.

"Hello," I said, touching once the drying mixture on my face.

"It's me," Kira said. "I was wondering if you had a second?"

I smiled, or at least I tried to. The mask I was wearing was making my skin tight. "Of course. I love to help."

"I know." Kira sighed. "Look, I'm sorry if I've been a pill lately. You know I've missed you as a Smitten Kitten. Without you, we just don't have that same pep."

That was sweet of her to say. It reminded me of how much I missed her. "Aw...thanks, K."

She laughed, sounding happy with my happiness. "So I guess what I'm saying is...I'll stand up for you, Tess. I want you on the squad. Full-time."

I straightened, completely caught off guard. It was the best thing I could've heard. I felt completely vindicated. "Really?"

"Yes," Kira said. "Being captain takes a lot of stuffing, and I'm just not sure I'm enough Kitten for it. I need more time for my life, my boyfriend. So I could use your help."

My eyes were beginning to tear, and I shot a glance over to Leona, who was still at my mirror applying oatmeal to her face with the back of a spoon.

"You have no idea what this means to me," I murmured. "Thank you."

"Course," Kira responded. "No one cheers like you, Tess. No one."

After we'd hung up, I put my phone back on the side table and sat down on my bed, wrapping my arms around my knees. Finally I had part of me back. I was going to be a Smitten Kitten again.

"What was that about?" Leona asked, turning to look at me through a face of oatmeal.

I met her gaze and smiled (sort of). "I'm back on the squad!"

Leona pursed her lips as she seemed to consider it, then she shrugged. "It's about time." Then she flipped over her wrist to look down at the watch she always wore. "Hey, I have to babysit my little sister tonight. I'll just keep this junk on my face until it falls off. My pores have been seriously neglected." She began walking to my bedroom door.

"No cucumbers?" I asked. She paused.

"I'll take a few for the road."

After Leona was gone, I decided to treat my eyelids to a little cucumber time of their own. I stretched out on my couch and closed my eyes, dropping two perfectly circular veggies on my eyes.

I was a cheerleader. I was a Smitten Kitten once again. And by golly, I hadn't realized how much I'd missed it.

I must have fallen asleep, because the sound of my doorbell startled me. I darted upright, the cucumbers falling off my eyes. I could see the sun setting out the window as I got up and began walking toward the door. The bell rang again.

When I got there, I pulled the door open, still a bit hazy from falling asleep. Joel gasped when he saw me.

"Holy shit, Tessa! You nearly gave me a heart attack."

I tried to pull my eyebrows together when I realized that I couldn't. My oatmeal and egg mask had hardened on my face, resulting in a look that was undeniably insane. "Oh my!" I yelled, running for the bathroom.

It took nearly ten minutes and a lot of hot water to get the concoction off my face, but when I looked up, my pink skin looked smooth as a baby's you-know-what. Overall, I was pleased.

When I came out, Joel was still near my door, but he had come in and shut it.

"Sorry," I said. He waved me off.

"No worries, I love horror movies." He smiled. "And I probably shouldn't have just shown up."

"True," I said, leaning against the counter. "And why again are you here?"

"To jump you," he said, and then his eyes got wide. "To jump your car. Your car needs the jump. Oh God." Joel rubbed his chin. "Have you gotten your car yet?" he asked.

"I have not."

"Would you like to? My plans for tonight got canceled, and I thought, 'Wow, fixing Tessa Crimson's car sounds like a great time!'"

"You thought that?" I knew he didn't, but I appreciated him

thinking of me. In fact, my day seemed to keep improving. I was glad I had Joel to share it with.

"Yeah," he said, like I'd asked a silly question. "Now let's go get greasy!" He rubbed his hands together like he was ready to get down to work.

Since my parents still weren't home, I decided to take him up on his offer for help. It was better than lying around with cucumbers on my eyes.

"Let me just change real quick," I said, motioning down to my beauty-ritual sweats. Joel nodded, and I dashed to my room.

I slid on a pair of jeans and a T-shirt and then slicked my hair back into a ponytail. I finished with some gloss. "Ready," I called as I came back in the room, grabbing my purse from next to the couch.

"Actually," Joel said, looking me over. "Since you look normal now, did you want to stop for a corn dog first?"

I scrunched my nose, thinking. I hadn't considered the issue of dinner.

"There's a fair in the parking lot of the mall. Wanna go?" he asked.

"The one where you can get killed on the rides?"

"Yep."

I laughed. They did have good corn dogs there. I considered it.

"I'll even take you on the super-slide," he said, nodding enthusiastically. "Twice!" He held up his fingers.

"Sold."

I adjusted my purse strap over my shoulder and followed him out of my house to his car. I wasn't sure why, but an evening at a fair sounded like a really great idea. In fact, it was the best idea of the night.

ASSIGNMENT 2

The operative watched from the booth as she sipped casually on a latte and slid on a pair of dark sunglasses. Tate and Jenn were across the way, in line for the mini–Ferris wheel. It seemed bold to go on a date to a very public local fair, but then again, cheating on your boyfriend wasn't exactly subtle.

Tate put his arm around Jenn, and after she took a cautionary glance around, she snuggled into his shoulder. The operative's stomach turned. It looked like Jenn's betrayal was finally going to happen. In a way, the operative had hoped that they would rethink the affair, especially since Jenn was the original one to order the investigation. But the operative knew all too well that it would be a one-hundred percent cheat confirmation—it had been ever since the first day SOS had started.

The operative took one more sip from her vanilla-flavored coffee before tossing it in the trash. She tapped her foot, waiting patiently for Tate and Jenn to move up in line. When it was their turn to board, she made her move.

Without drawing any suspicion, she stalked across the paved ground and stepped up behind them, just close enough to drop a chip into Jenn's oversized beach bag. Once it was released, the operative smiled and moved back, watching them get in the cart. Neither suspect turned.

It took a minute for the next cart to arrive. When it did, the operative climbed into its purple steel cage. From where she was, she could see Tate and Jenn nestled closely together. The ride began to spin slowly, swooping them up into the sky.

The operative slid the earbud in and put her finger over it to listen. With her other hand, she pointed a small camera in their direction. She'd already caught one pair of cheaters. Now it was going to be two for two. And then she'd outshine Tessa in every way.

"I don't want to hide anymore," Jenn whispered, looking up into Tate's face. "I want to be with you."

"Oh my God," the operative murmured, shaking her head. Jenn just went from flirt to full-fledged cheater in three seconds flat. She was amazed at the lack of remorse.

Tate smiled widely, leaning down to softly touch his lips to Jenn's, just a peck. "Babe," he breathed as he stayed close to her face. "I want you too."

They stayed together like that for a full turn of the Ferris wheel as the operative gritted her teeth, both excited and sickened by the culmination of it all. She zoomed in to capture their tender kisses.

"What am I going to tell Riley?" Jenn asked, reaching up to play with Tate's hair.

"Tell him you're in love with me."

Jenn shook her head. "That's cruel." She sighed. "Maybe I'll break up with him, and then we can wait a week or something so it doesn't look suspicious."

The operative scoffed. Oh, now they were going to lie about being together? They were disgusting. She began tapping her foot, almost feverishly.

"I don't want to wait a week," Tate whispered, kissing her again.

"I can't believe I stayed with him so long. I should have been with you," Jenn said, her hand sliding suspiciously lower into the seat of the cart.

"Slut," the operative called out, her anger too much to suppress.

Jenn sat up straighter, swinging her head around, but the operative put her cell phone to her ear to pretend like she was on the phone and not paying attention. After a minute, Jenn turned back around, looking a little less comfortable in Tate's arms. The operative smiled, enjoying Jenn's reaction. In fact, the more she thought about it, the more reaction she wanted. She considered how she could make things right. What sort of...revenge she could have.

Tapping her nails on the steel seat of the Ferris wheel cart, the operative turned to look out over the parking lot, wishing the ride would stop. She was hungry. Spying sometimes did that to her. She gazed over to the food tents and—

The operative flinched when she saw her—Tessa Crimson, walking by the rows of games, laughing. But she wasn't alone. She was walking with a guy.

Reaching to get her camera, the operative zoomed in on their faces. Tessa's smooth features were perfect as always. Her dark, shiny hair was pulled back into a perky ponytail, flowing down behind her shoulders. Her wide smile flashed, not only drawing attention from the guy she was with, but from the filthy fair workers watching her.

The operative moved her lens, taking in the face of Tessa's companion. It took a second from that height before she recognized him. It was *Joel Fletcher*! She gasped as she scanned him from head to toe. His hazel eyes were set off nicely against his light skin. He had on a vintage-rocker T-shirt and a faded pair of loose jeans that completed his look.

The operative clenched her jaw. "Again?" she whispered, her voice nearly a growl. As if one cheating friend wasn't enough, now there was Tessa Crimson with an attached guy—eating a corn dog!

Was Tessa the ultimate cheating accomplice? Getting away with it all by being perky and cute. Slipping under the radar. Narrowing her eyes, the operative aimed the camera at the two of them, clicking off shot after shot until she ran out of film. She wouldn't stand for this.

No, Tessa Crimson was going down.

When the Ferris wheel stopped, the operative climbed out, her fist clenching the strap of the satchel over her shoulder. Heading toward the parking lot, she thought about the best way to take Tessa down. She didn't need proof this time. Tessa was a repeat offender—she'd already been through this with Christian.

About halfway across the concrete she paused, remembering the mission she'd just accomplished. Jenn and Tate.

It took a minute to find it, but when she spotted Jenn's Honda Accord, she wasted no time. She stomped over to it, darting around cautionary glances. When no one was near, she squatted and took a metal letter opener out of her bag. She gripped it in one hand and drove it into the smooth part of the driver's-side tire. She twisted and turned the blade, her face pulled into a snarl.

There was a hiss as the air escaped from the rubber. The operative pulled out her weapon and slid it back into her satchel as she straightened up. She doubted that Jenn knew how to change a tire. And depending on the kind of guy Tate was, he might not know either.

With that, she brought a business card out of her back pocket, kissed it, and put it in the jamb of the driver's-side window.

Now it was time to catch a Kitten.

CHAPTER SIXTEEN

"THIS LOOKS DISGUSTING." I LAUGHED, TWIRLING the corn dog stick in my hand.

"Come on." Joel knocked his elbow into mine as we walked across the fairgrounds. "Hot dogs covered in batter and shoved on a stick? It's like the most delicious combination on the planet."

I didn't mind coming here with Joel. I was really enjoying it. Even though Kira, Leona, Izzie, and the other girls on the squad were great, I really missed having a guy around. Not in a boyfriend way, but just that male presence. In fact, it was nice to not have to worry about the boyfriend baggage.

"So Kira told me she was going to put you back on the squad," Joel said as we passed the Ferris wheel. "Did she?"

"Yep. I am officially a Smitten Kitten, a member of the fiercest squad in Washington."

"Ah," Joel said. "Taking your rightful place at the helm soon, hopefully." He finished his corn dog and tossed the stick in the trash as we passed it. "It'd be a good thing," he added. "I was starting to think that Kira was going to lose her mind with all the practices and infighting. You all are a feisty bunch!"

I pursed my lips and then nodded. "Yeah, but we love each other."

"So sweet," Joel cooed, placing his hand over his heart.

"Zip your lip!"

"Wait." Joel took my arm and pulled me sideways. "We have to go see this!"

"What?" I followed him as he dragged me over to the haunted house, which was really a renovated trailer. "They might have real ax-wielding murderers in there," I said, raising my eyebrow.

"Don't worry," he whispered as he paid the carnie in tickets. "I'm a trained assassin."

"Wow."

"Yep. Deadly. Ninja-like reflexes."

I laughed and walked into the haunted house behind him, pausing to throw out my half-eaten corn dog before going in.

The haunted house was a bit of a letdown. The cart stalled out once, stranding us in a small room among a sea of glowing red eyes. Only most of the bulbs had burned out, so there was just a lot of winking lights going on. Despite the non-scare factor, Joel made bad jokes the entire time, so it was sort of fun.

And after about two hours and *three* rides on the super-slide, I was exhausted—filled with confectionary sugar and ready to go. We were halfway to his car (still needing to jump my own) when my phone vibrated in my pocket.

"It's Kira," I said, looking down at it as I pulled it out. "Tell her I say hi," Joel replied, reaching into his jeans to take out his car keys.

The minute I clicked on the phone and put it to my ear, Kira started talking.

"We're at the gymnasium," she said in a monotone. "You need to meet us here."

"Oh..." I looked over at Joel, surprised by Kira's tone. "Did something—"

"And bring Joel with you," Kira interrupted, and then hung up.

My breath caught and I stopped walking, pulling the phone slowly from my ear to look at it. Guilt consumed me.

"Everything okay?" Joel asked, clicking the locks of his car. I brought my eyes to his soft hazel ones, wondering if I'd done something wrong.

"She wants me to meet her at the gym," I said, swallowing hard.

"Cool. Your car is parked there anyway. I'll drop you off."

"Actually," I said, moving past him to his passenger door. "She wants to see both of us."

Joel looked back at me, then shrugged and walked around the front of his car to his door. He might not look fazed, but something in Kira's voice worried me. And I had a feeling the fair might not have been a good idea after all.

Kira shifted on her sneakered feet, glaring at me as we walked into the gymnasium. Then she softened her eyes and looked to Joel. "Hi, honey," she said with exaggerated sweetness as her voice echoed across the court. "I've been wondering where you were." She was smiling, but I could tell by the shallowness of her dimples that it was forced.

"Hey." Joel left my side and walked across the gymnasium to Kira, kissing her cheek when he got there. He'd fixed my car before we came in just in case. In case of what, I wasn't sure. "It took a while," Joel told Kira. "Tessa needed a jump."

Leona coughed at his word choice.

He darted a glance at her before continuing. "Then I figured since I had to bring her back here, I'd stop by the fair at the mall and get a corn dog."

"You're so adorable," Kira said, reaching up to pet his chin. I felt a small twinge of discomfort.

The gym doors swung open and Izzie came running in. "Girls," she called. "There's something you have to see...." She stopped in her tracks, noticing Joel. "Oh. Hi, Joel," she said, looking between him and the rest of the squad.

He laughed. "Where's the fire, Izzie?"

Izzie took her hair in her hand and twisted, a sure sign of her nervousness. "It..." I could tell she was struggling to find an answer.

"Is that the new jacket you wanted from Hollister?" Kira interrupted, her eyes narrowed slightly.

"Yes," Izzie snapped, sighing. "The jacket. Isn't it great?"

Joel nodded, not catching on in the slightest. Normally I would have politely asked him to leave, but judging by Kira's protective hand on his bicep, it wasn't my place. And I had a feeling that she was already pretty ticked at me.

"Mind if I meet you after practice?" she asked him, flicking her eyes toward me once. I lowered my head.

"That's cool," he said. "Call me when you're done and I'll pick you up."

They embraced quickly, and I felt further out of place. I wrapped my arms around myself in a hug. When they separated, Joel waved to the other girls and walked past me on the way to the exit.

"And thanks for hanging out, Tess. It was really fun." His smile was innocent, friendly. But I could practically feel the daggers coming my way from Kira.

"Bye," I said casually, not returning his compliment.

Pressing his lips together and raising his eyebrows in a "what's up" gesture, Joel raised his hand to me and crossed to the double doors. I regretted not being able to return his enthusiasm, but I could feel the hot water boiling around me. When Joel was gone, I looked over at Kira.

She was watching me, twisting a blonde curl around her finger. Her eyes were wide and innocent, but I knew Kira. That expression was hiding something underneath.

"Are you upset with me?" I asked, walking toward her.

She laughed, dropping her arms at her sides. "Of course not. Why would I be mad? You're Tessa. So you get your pick, right?"

I gasped. Leona mumbled something I couldn't quite catch before walking to the bleachers.

"Kira!" Was she implying that I was trying to steal her boyfriend? That was completely uncalled for! I put my fists on my hips. "What do you mean by that?"

"Izzie," she said, holding out her hand. "Can you give me the pictures again?"

"Sure." Izzie sounded absolutely defeated. "There was also an update on the blog," she whispered. She darted a glance at me and then pulled a few glossy pages of pictures from her backpack. She marched over and handed them to Kira, peering over her shoulder.

"Oh, look," Kira said sarcastically. "You're super-photogenic, Tess!" She jutted out her hand, the papers flapping. I took them from her and looked down.

TGI Friday's! Someone had been spying on me! I swallowed hard as I sorted through the pictures. They were from the fair, when I was with Joel. Only, the way the pictures looked, I was *with* Joel.

There were several frames of us staring at each other, laughing. Even the moment when he had to reach over to wipe a bit of whipped cream off my chin. We looked rather...cozy.

"It's not what it seems," I said, glancing up at Kira.

She watched me for a minute, seeming to think it over. "Someone dropped these in an unmarked envelope taped to my front door a little while ago." She sighed, maybe suddenly recognizing that I hadn't actually done anything wrong. "Either way, it's obvious that you're their target," she said. "I think it's time you start keeping a lower profile, Tess. Maybe Mary was right. Maybe the Smitten Kittens aren't for you after all."

The annoyance in her voice was palpable. She turned toward the bleachers, picking at her manicure.

"You can't just take it back like that," I called to her.

She spun to face me. "Can't I?"

"Wait," Leona said, holding up her finger. I was happy someone was going to stick up for me. "This can be a good thing."

"It is?" Kira asked, looking over her shoulder at her. I glared at Leona, unsure how my dismissal from the squad could ever be a positive thing.

"Not the Smitten Kitten stuff." Leona shook her head. "The spying on Tessa. We can use it. Use it to lure out the copy-Kitten. And I have an idea," she added, starting to smile at me. "But it's kinda crazy."

"How crazy?" I asked, my heart beginning to speed up at the look of excitement on Leona's face. If anyone could make sense of the situation, it was Leona. She was amazingly logical.

"Faked affair," she said, nodding and licking at her teeth. "One between you and Joel."

"Oh, that sounds brilliant," Kira snapped fiercely. "My boyfriend is not a pawn in your game of checkers."

"It's chess, you dumb blonde. Now *what* is your deal?" Leona shouted at her, standing up. "You've been a total bitch since becoming captain. Do you have chronic PMS or what?"

"Um." Izzie raised her hand. "PMS is a real condition. I don't think we should joke about it."

"Shut up!" both Leona and Kira said to her at the same time. I gasped. Were my Kittens about to tango?

Kira straightened and then climbed atop a bleacher so that she stood a foot higher than Leona. "You don't know anything," Kira hissed at her.

"You mean, other than the fact that your insecurities are making you a jealous maniac? And I'm not just talking about Joel here."

"Leona," I scolded, marching over to them.

"Stay out of this, Tessa," Kira said without looking at me. I stopped, staring at her. But Kira was going skirt to skirt with Leona, locked in some ancient art of intimidation.

"She's our true captain," Leona said through a clenched jaw. It made me think they'd had this conversation before—maybe about me getting back on the squad.

"Doesn't mean I have to stand by and watch it."

"Watch what?" My heart was pounding in my chest. I felt like I was coming in late to an argument, but I'd been here from the start. From the start of everything.

Both Kira and Leona ignored me for a minute, and then Kira dropped her head. "Whatever," she said, waving her hand. "Do what you want, but count me out. I'm not putting my boyfriend up for grabs for the sake of Tessa's reputation."

Before Leona could respond, Kira hopped down from the bleachers and grabbed up her backpack from the gym floor. She looked up once and met my eyes.

"Sorry," she said to me, her blue eyes glassy. "I'm not trying to hurt your feelings, Tess. But...you know what they say." She put her pack over her shoulder. "Keep your friends close, but your best friends even closer."

"It's enemies."

She pressed her lips together in a sad smile. "Exactly."

And then she turned around and walked out of the gymnasium.

I flinched like I'd been slapped across the face. I looked over at Izzie, who was watching me wide-eyed, unsure of who to follow. Luckily she stayed where she was.

"Well, that was fun," Leona muttered, climbing down from the wood bench and smoothing out her skirt. "Can we talk about how the hell we're going to catch this copy-Kitten now? I have a strongly worded letter that I need to write."

The plan was simple, really. The weekend after next was the homecoming dance, the primo event for Washington High—a time when relationships (and affairs) were forged. Since the copy-Kitten was so interested in me, even when I wasn't a subject, they'd surely be interested in investigating me for real, now that I was officially named.

Leona would send in a cheater request form pretending to be Kira and name Joel and me as the targets. The tough part was going to be trying to pull this off without letting Joel in on our plan. Surely he couldn't know that the Smitten Kittens were SOS, or rather the real SOS.

I would just have to be seen with him. We'd considered setting something up for Chris's party on Saturday, but Kira had told us that Joel wouldn't be there. I admit, I was a little disappointed. After seeing Aiden with Mary, the thought of another date with Chris made me slightly nauseous. It would have been nice to see a friendly face.

So we decided that the best place for Operation Knockoff would be at homecoming, with Joel and me in a compromised position. And even though Kira refused to participate in the sting or talk to me other than in short sentences, she was still up for going to Chris's party on Saturday with us.

However awkward that might be.

SOS
CHEATER REQUEST

CASE: 005
CLIENT: Kira Reynolds
SUBJECT: Joel Fletcher

Due to the sensitive nature of this assignment, we will keep this notice brief. SOS will be investigating Tessa Crimson, free of charge, in the suspected cheat of Joel Fletcher.

Although pictures were supplied already, from your sternly worded letter, we gather that you're not ready to accept this crime.

Because of that, SOS will confirm the cheat and provide revenge tactics.

SOS will inform you of our findings as soon as possible. We would also recommend that you no longer associate with Ms. Crimson or the Smitten Kittens.

Keep kicking ass,
SOS ☺
SOS
www.thecheaterreports.blogspot.com
Text: 555-1863
Exposing Cheaters for Over Three Years

CHAPTER SEVENTEEN

"HURRY UP, LEONA," KIRA CALLED FROM THE driver's seat as Leona walked out the front double doors of her huge brick house. Her dad's vintage cars were in the driveway, making her already-impressive house that much more eclectic.

We'd parked on her street, sitting at the curb for close to fifteen minutes while we waited for her. But the second I saw her, I knew why. She looked delicious. Her brown hair had been set in curlers, leaving it all wavy, with her fringed bangs brushed to the side. She'd gotten new contacts and lined her eyes heavily with liner, giving her that model-just-out-of-rehab look. Her black minidress with strappy heels was a total ensemble!

Izzie whistled from the passenger seat as Leona climbed into the back with me. I smiled.

"You look ravishing," I said, reaching up to touch one of her curls.

She shrugged. "No big deal."

"It certainly is," Kira announced before checking her mirrors and pulling out into the street. "You finally look like a real Kitten."

Not true. Leona always looked like herself, which was exactly right for a Smitten Kitten. But Kira and I were only speaking to each other when necessary, and contradicting her right now didn't qualify as necessary.

"Shove it, Kira," Leona said, reaching over to adjust the strap on her sandals. "I just wanted to put myself back on the market. Worry about your own boyfriend."

"When were you off the market?" Kira laughed. "And don't worry about Joel. He's just fine."

Leona shot me a glance, then turned to look out the back window at the passing trees. "Let's drop it. I'm just ready to have fun. That's all."

After the week I'd had, I was hoping that Chris's party would be more on the hook than off, but I was wrong. There were at least twenty people standing on the front lawn of his two-story, red Craftsman's-style home. A few were playing horseshoes (which I'm sure the neighbors loved), and some were just sitting on the porch watching and drinking, occasionally calling out winners.

Kira bumped the curb as she parked in front, causing the crowd to taunt us.

"Nice," Leona murmured. I could see the splotches of red appearing on her neck and chest. It wasn't a common thing for Leona to look petrified.

Izzie sighed longingly from the front seat. "I bet Sam liked horseshoes."

"He probably did," I said, trying to be supportive. Then I leaned over and pushed open the door. As the rest of the girls filtered out, grouping around me, I became uncomfortably aware that I was underdressed.

Leona was in a minidress, and Kira and Izzie were both in short skirts and ballet flats. I, however, was wearing a white T-shirt with jeans and sandals. They seemed to notice my clothes too.

"Jeez, Tessa, could you have even tried to impress Chris?"

Kira said, fluffing her blonde curls. "I could have let you borrow an outfit."

I wasn't sure if Kira was trying to be friendly or if she was putting me down because she was still upset about the Joel misunderstanding. Either way, I decided to just be polite.

"Thanks for the offer."

"Let's go," Leona said, looping her arm in mine and heading across the soft grass and toward the party. A few people said hi to me as we walked. I sensed that just by being here, I was getting part of my reputation back. Although at this point, I wasn't really sure how much I cared.

The music was loud. Really loud. We wandered in, Izzie and Kira immediately heading to the kitchen in search of cups while Leona and I decided to stake out the scene from the living room.

We stood by the fireplace and scanned the room.

"Do you think the copy-Kitten is here?" I asked, swallowing hard. It made goose bumps rise on my arms, just thinking about being watched. Again.

"Naw," Leona said. "I doubt it, since Joel's not here." She turned to me. "But then again, you seem to be the flavor of the week, so there is a chance she's tracking you."

"Reassuring." I felt my phone vibrate in my jeans pocket and held it up to check the number. I drew in a harsh breath. "It's Mary," I murmured.

"Shit."

"Language."

"Sorry, Tess." But then Leona reached for my phone, plucking it from my hands and putting it to her ear. "Tessa's phone," she said into it, looking sideways at me.

Her carefully lined eyes narrowed. "Yeah, see, Mary, I don't think Tessa's all that keen on talking to you right now. Why?" Leona laughed, reaching up to switch the phone to her other ear. "Maybe because you're a sneaky bitch? Maybe because we saw you kiss her boyfriend—ex, whatever. Doesn't matter. You violated Smitten Kitten code."

There was a mix of sickness and relief in my stomach. I didn't want it said so bluntly about Mary and Aiden. Saying it made it real. But then again, I was just so glad to have Leona stick up for me. I hadn't felt protected in a long time.

Leona sighed. "Sure," she said. "I'll tell her. Bye." Leona pulled the phone from her face and looked at it as she clicked it off, averting her eyes.

"Tell me what?" I asked, my heart racing.

Leona pressed her lips together and turned, holding my phone out to me. "She said she's sorry and that she didn't mean for it to happen."

Grief rushed through me. It was the only way to describe the ache that pulled at my ribs, making my lip quiver.

"Listen," Leona said. "I know this isn't the time, but I think Mary may be my main suspect."

"I thought you said it was Chloe," I mumbled, sniffling once. I hated to cry off my makeup, but I wasn't sure I could hold it in. My phone vibrated again in my hand, and when I turned it over, I saw Aiden's mother's number.

Was his mom calling me or was he in town? I clicked it off, sending it to voice mail before shoving it deep into my pants pocket.

"Aiden?" Leona asked. When I nodded, she slung her arm over my shoulders. "Figures. Mary probably just called him and told him that you—" She stopped as I noticeably tensed. "Never mind," she said. "I'm sure they totally don't talk on the phone or anything."

Just then there were some cheers from across the room. I looked up to see Chris come in, dressed in his jersey. Looking very…athletic. A few of his teammates began chanting his name, and he held up his beer cup in greeting, but it was obvious where his attention was focused. On me. I gulped and looked away toward the front window.

"Straighten up," Leona said, adjusting her own posture. I blew out a breath, pushing away the painful thoughts of Aiden and Mary. I needed to try to accept my destiny as a Smitten Kitten and what was right for me. I glanced up to see Chris standing there, beaming with his perfectly straight teeth.

"I can't believe you came," he said, reaching up to brush self-consciously at his blond hair. "You look great."

I would have thought he was just trying to be polite, but his blue eyes looked positively honest as he gazed at me.

"Right," Leona said with a laugh. "I think Tessa's T-shirt is from this year's Balenciaga collection."

Chris looked over at her, seeming confused. I smiled.

"It was a joke," Leona muttered, shaking her head.

"It was funny," I assured her, pulling down on the hem of my shirt to iron out some of the wrinkles. I really should have worn something a little dressier.

"Obviously," she said back, and glanced around the crowded room. "Okay," she said with a long breath. "I'm going to find Kira and Izzie and get a drink. You two"—she looked between us— "have a blast."

"Thanks!" Chris and I answered at the same time and then looked at each other somewhat awkwardly.

"Good luck with that." Leona widened her eyes, then eased her way through the bodies in the room toward the kitchen.

Once she was gone, Chris moved forward to rest his muscular arm on the mantel of the fireplace. His biceps were huge—he didn't even have to flex. I relaxed a little.

"The party's great," I said, having to talk a little louder than was comfortable for being this close. "I think the entire school is here."

"Only the seniors," he said. "Trying to play the role, you know." He smiled at me. "Stuck-up jock."

I laughed. "And the cheerleader." I pointed to myself. "How cliché."

"I did have to turn away a few juniors earlier. It was sort of fun, although I know it's not nice to say being a dick is fun."

I flinched. Juniors? "Who'd you turn away?"

Chris exhaled, leaning closer to me as he scratched at his head. "Um...Johnny Rake, Giselle...somebody, Chloe Ferril—"

"Wait," I said, holding up my hand. "Chloe Ferril was here?" I spun around the room, my Kitten senses tingling, as I looked for the other members of my squad.

"Yeah..." Chris said. "She was here, all gothed out. Why? You two still don't like each other?"

"I have to go," I answered, turning back to him suddenly. The disappointment on his face was plain and I felt awful. But...if Leona's original thoughts were correct, Chloe could be the copy-Kitten. And she might still be here!

With a quick apologetic smile, I turned to move away. A moment later, one of the defensive linemen ran in from the hallway. He swung his thick neck around until he found Chris and then grinned.

"Dude," he called. "Check your e-mail!"

"Why?" Chris asked, stepping forward and touching my arm casually. My back tensed.

"Cheaters, man! Everyone's getting a video of cheaters!"

Just then, my phone vibrated in my pocket, tickling my leg. A second later, I heard Chris's phone go off next to me—the ring tone of Washington High's fight song. I would have been impressed, but at the same moment, several other phones began ringing. A mix of buzzing, dinging, and top-forty hits.

I gasped, my fingers trembling.

"What the hell?" Chris asked, taking out his phone and looking at it. I was too scared to look at mine. "Someone's streaming a video."

I stepped over and put my hand on Chris's arm as I leaned in to look at his screen. There was an hourglass turning, loading a video. Glancing around the living room, I saw that everyone who had a phone was looking at it, and those who didn't were sharing.

I held my breath, grasping Chris's warm skin, not caring that I wasn't into him. Not caring that not being into him might mean I couldn't be a Smitten Kitten. Because whatever I was about to see, it would be bad. I could feel it in my pom-poms.

The hourglass faded, the screen showing a still from outside a window, looking into a classroom. Wait. Was that the music room? The image focused in on someone dashing into the room. It zoomed in.

I reached out to pull Chris's phone closer to us. Riley Richards? Oh, frack! This couldn't be good.

"Shit, Riley!" Chris called out teasingly, glancing into the party. "It's you!" He pointed.

I looked up, seeing Riley standing in the middle of the room with his girlfriend, Jenn, his eyes widening at the mention of his name. Obviously *he* hadn't gotten the call.

Jenn's eyes darted around the room. "What?" she asked, laughing nervously.

I bit down hard on my lip and turned back to the phone. Riley was still in the music room, and I hoped that possibly, this was just a joke. But it wasn't.

Megan Wright walked into the music room, going immediately to Riley, pausing uncomfortably close. I peeked at Jenn as she looked from person to person, wanting to know what we were seeing. Finally she ran over to Fredrick Henry and snatched his iPhone out of his hand.

"Hey!" he yelled, but Jenn was already staring at the screen, her lip curling. It reminded me of how freaked out Megan was when I saw her in the hallway that day. Wait. Was that when this was shot?

"Is Megan here?" I whispered to Chris, tilting my head toward his.

He furrowed his brow as if thinking and then shook his head. "Don't think so."

"Good."

The music had stopped and the party was quiet, other than a few expletives and snickers. My throat was dry with anxiety. This copy-Kitten had seriously crossed the line. This was a heinous violation of privacy! No one—not even a cheater—should be exposed like this.

"Nice, Riley!" someone called from across the room. "Megan's hot." Riley didn't look up; he kept his eyes trained on the ground, his face colorless.

I blinked quickly, my heart thudding. On the screen Riley and Megan were whispering to each other, and then, they got closer.

"Make out! Make out!" a football player started yelling, soon getting the entire room to chant.

"Slippery eel," I murmured, looking around the room. The copy-Kitten had no idea the damage she was inflicting, both for the victims and for SOS. Jenn lowered the phone, holding it away from her like it was poisonous.

"Megan!" she screamed loud enough to make me jump. "My best fucking friend?"

Riley didn't look up at her. He was still, like a statue, taking slow breaths.

The screen on the phone went black, and I thought it was over when another video began. "Oh, no," I whispered, wondering how much worse it would get.

At first, I couldn't understand the picture. The camera was shaking, moving amid blue and red flashes. Then I saw some people gathered below. "Is that—"

"The mall fair," Chris said, turning to me. "I was going to see if you wanted to go the other night."

Sigh. It was nice of him to think of me. I was about to smile when it occurred to me. Would I be on the next tape? My word, I was about to get exposed to the entire school even though I hadn't actually done anything wrong!

"We've got another one!" someone yelled.

My body immediately tensed, and I looked over at Chris's phone. On the video the camera zoomed in, focusing on a steel cart of what looked like a Ferris wheel. Definitely the fair. Rock, paper, scissors! This was it.

But instead of me, I saw Jenn, her short dark hair blowing in the breeze. She was a cart ahead on the ride. She was talking with someone. Then she smiled and moved to press her mouth on a guy. I didn't recognize him, but he certainly wasn't Riley. My word. It was a double cheat!

The screen went blank, and then words appeared, scrolling across the screen.

You've just been busted by SOS.

I put my hand over my mouth, surprised. I felt horrified by the tactic, yet relieved that I wasn't on the tape. Even though the copy-Kitten had definitely thought I'd done something wrong, she hadn't outed me. I tilted my head, considering that.

"You pig!"

My eyes snapped up in time to see Jenn slap (really hard) Riley high up on his cheek. He stumbled back, holding his face, and narrowed his eyes at her.

"Me? And what the fuck were you doing, Jenn? Was he choking? Were you giving him CPR?"

Chris snorted from next to me but straightened up when I looked sideways at him. Watching this scene was way too intimate, yet I couldn't turn away.

Jenn's face twisted, and then she reached up to brush her hair away from her face. "She's my best friend," she whispered harshly. "You were screwing my best friend."

"No, I wasn't." Riley shook his head. "It wasn't like that."

"Oh, shit. It's Tate!" Jordan Prichard (captain of the football team) called, pointing toward the doorway of Chris's house.

Tate's eyes widened at the mention of his name, and he raised his chin in greeting. His face softened when he saw Jenn, and he opened his mouth to say something to her. But Riley was off.

In about one point three seconds, he had Tate on the floor, beating on him.

"Stop it!" Jenn screamed, running over to try to pry her boyfriend off of her...other boyfriend.

It was mayhem. People were cheering, both guys and girls, but no one was stopping the fight. Jenn's mascara had begun running down her face, streaking her like a scorned prom queen, and Tate covered his head as Riley continued to hit him.

"Stop them!" I yelled at Chris, pushing his arm in that direction.

"Let them fight," he said, sounding completely jock. "They need to get it out."

My mouth opened in disgust. That was a horrible idea! And I should know. I got hit in the head with a clock last year during a fight!

Well, this just wouldn't do. I stomped over, grabbing a beer out of Deon Mosely's hand, and pushed my way toward the three cheaters struggling on the floor. When I got to the front of the wrestlers, I threw the cup of beer at them.

Everyone gasped at once, and from the corner of my eye, I saw the Smitten Kittens run in from the kitchen. Leona laughed, nodding proudly. Izzie covered her mouth, looking terrified, and Kira stood there, a blank expression on her face. She probably didn't think it was very SK of me to toss alcoholic beverages on people, but I felt justified.

"What the frig?" Jenn yelled at me, her white blouse soaked, showing the lace of her pink bra underneath.

Riley was still sitting on Tate, but he was panting loudly as he stared at his girlfriend, beer dripping from his head. Tate's eyes were closed, his face covered in microbrew, but his hands were pinned, making it impossible for him to wipe it away.

Then the strangest thing happened. Like—totally and freakishly unexpected. Riley reached out to grab Jenn and pull himself to her. He hugged her tight, tucking her head against his chest as he brushed at her wet hair.

"I'm sorry," he murmured. "I'm so sorry."

I dropped the plastic cup to the floor with a ping and watched them. Watched as Jenn drew back, touching Riley's face, wiping off the liquid. Tate was still lying on the floor, stunned.

Jenn started to sob. "I love you."

"I love you too." Riley buried his head against her shoulder as he began to cry, shaking from it. The crowd murmured, then began to dissipate as someone turned the music back on. But I stayed, unsure of what had just happened.

"What the hell?" I heard, and turned to see Kira standing next to me.

"Language," I said.

"Heck. Now…are they not breaking up? Someone just told me that SOS sent out a video of both of them cheating."

"Not SOS. Fake SOS."

"Whatever," she said, putting her hands on her hips as she studied the couple.

"They must have realized they were still in love," Leona called, coming to stand on the other side of Kira. "Like seeing the cheating made them want each other back. Not sure. But it sounds sick and twisted."

"It's totally understandable!" Izzie said, reaching out to touch my shoulder as she stood next to me. "If I saw Sam cheat, I'd still want him back."

I swung to face her. "That's not a good thing," I said. "That's not love. And Oprah would not approve." I sighed. After my time away from the squad, I felt like all of us had lost a little self-esteem. "Iz," I said. "We're going to rebuild your inner Kitten. Understand?"

She blinked her round green eyes at me and nodded once to show she understood. I turned back to see Tate slowly getting up. His bottom lip was a little puffed, but otherwise it looked like most of the damage was superficial. He stared after the couple, his face looking contorted, sad.

Then he glanced out at the party, people going back to their lives now that the fight was over. His eyes met mine for a second, and I felt it. The loneliness. He did love Jenn. But she didn't choose him. She chose her boyfriend.

Before I could smile my support, he turned and limped toward the door and out into the dark Washington night. I sighed heavily, about to turn away, when I saw him.

My entire body reacted. Aiden was standing out on the lawn of Chris's house, dressed in a wrinkled tracksuit, his short hair messy. He held up his hand in a wave, looking solemn.

I blinked back the burning in my eyes but couldn't look away from him. He was here for me. He had come to see me.

"Is that—" Kira stopped, her head snapping toward mine. I could feel her stare on my cheek. "What are you going to do?" she asked. Her words hung in the air because I wasn't sure how to answer.

"Go talk to him," Leona murmured. "Guy looks pathetic." She glanced back over her shoulder and then leaned forward to whisper to me. "I'll distract Chris."

I nodded, not caring what she did with Chris. Aiden was outside. And I had no idea what to say to him.

SOS
CHEATER CONFIRMATION

CASES: 001 and 002
CLIENT: Riley Richards and Jenn Duarte
STATUS: Case closed

This is a notice that the cases against Riley Richards and Jenn Duarte have been completed and closed.

Both were confirmed cheaters and both were exposed. The fact that they stayed together, and made out at Chris Townsend's party, is beside the point.

One of the accomplices, Megan Wright, has decided to switch schools, which we feel is for the best.

Remember, cheaters never win. Especially with SOS on the case.

Keep kicking ass,
SOS ☺
SOS
www.thecheaterreports.blogspot.com
Text: 555-1863
Exposing Cheaters for Over Three Years

CHAPTER EIGHTEEN

AIDEN WAS STANDING THERE IN THE GRASS WITH sneakers and running pants, looking natural—the way I loved him. Or at least, the way I used to love him.

He looked me up and down, and when his green eyes met mine, I could see how sincerely sorry he was. "Can we talk?" he asked.

I looked back at the house party, glad I'd shut the door when I walked out. I didn't need to become tonight's second show. And I didn't want anyone to see my heart break. Shoot, even I didn't want to witness that.

Walking across the soft grass, I stopped in front of Aiden, my lip already trying to quiver. But I tightened my mouth so that it wouldn't. Looking at him after actually witnessing him kiss another girl...it was a surreal moment. Like maybe this was all a dream. I nodded, letting him know he could talk.

"You look pretty," Aiden said quietly, bending his head toward mine. "I always liked you dressed down like this."

I wrapped my arms around myself, unable to blink away the tears before they fell. He wasn't allowed to compliment me.

"I should have told you about Mary," he said, his handsome face breaking. "I'm so sorry, baby."

There was a stabbing pain in my chest, and I stared down at the grass, wishing I could just sink into it and forget about Aiden and Mary. I hated her name in his mouth. I hated *her* in his mouth.

"I never wanted to hurt you or lie to you. I never meant to—"

"How long have you been dating her?" I asked, my voice croaking from the choked-back tears. I wouldn't look up at him. I couldn't.

He sniffled. "A month."

I gasped, stepping back from him, my hand at my neck. "A *month*?" But it only came out in a whisper. "Aiden, a *month*!" I covered my face with both hands, unable to keep it together. All the time he'd been with me, making out and cuddling, he'd been dating her. He was with somebody else. It hurt too much to comprehend. "Did she know? Did she know you and I were…"

His arms were around me, holding me. His warm whispers were in my ear, saying he was sorry. But I just cried. I didn't hug him back. I didn't reach for him.

"Tessa," he murmured, his hand protectively at the back of my neck. "I'll do anything. Please, I'm so sorry. I love you."

I choked, gasping for air as I pulled back to look up at him. "What?" I breathed. "What did you say?"

Aiden's face was streaked with tears, his normally green eyes now red. "I love you, baby. I love you so much. Please." He reached up to touch my arms, but I couldn't react. I didn't know how.

"You can't hate me, Tess," he pleaded. "You're my everything. I need you."

Confusion pulsed through me. "I saw you," I murmured. "I saw you kiss her."

"I know." His voice cracked. "And once that happened, I broke it off with Mary. I promise you. I don't know what I was thinking. It was just…Mary was at school, she was there. And in a way, it was like being with you, Tess. Especially since things between us had been so weird—"

"Oh my word," I squeaked, and backed out of his hands. The realization hit me. "Aiden, did you…did you *sleep* with her?" Please no. Please no.

His breath was jagged. As the boy I'd loved since the moment I met him stared back at me and nodded, everything left me. Everything I ever cared for was suddenly ruined. I felt…completely betrayed. Completely alone.

Aiden started saying something, but I wasn't listening anymore. I was looking past him, into the street. I wanted to go home.

"I love you." He kept saying it, as if it made everything else go away. As if it exonerated him. Or Mary.

I narrowed my eyes, thinking of her. Thinking of how her sneaking behind my back made her the ultimate snake. How she tried to ruin the Smitten Kittens for me. She was the fake SOS. If she could ruin my (sort of) relationship, she could ruin SOS.

"I'll do anything, Tess. Please."

On the corner, I saw a sedan turn onto the street. It was a sensible car. Something reliable. It slowed down just as it passed under a streetlight and I saw him. Immediately I smiled in relief, and suddenly I could breathe again. It was Joel.

Without a word to Aiden, I ran past him, my sandals slapping against my heels. I ran right into the road and put up my hands to stop the car. Joel braked violently and peered out of his windshield until he realized it was me.

He leaned his head out the driver's-side window. "Holy hell, Tessa. Are you trying to get killed?"

I laughed then, shaking my head. I was so relieved to see him that I didn't care that he almost ran me over. I was ready to go home.

"Tessa?" I heard Aiden call from the lawn behind me, but I didn't turn. I couldn't look at him right now. There was no such thing as Aiden.

"I need a ride, Joel," I said, rubbing absently at my low back. "I just really need a ride home right now."

Joel looked past me toward Aiden in the grass. He understood. "Get in."

I exhaled and started walking around the car. But before I climbed in, I looked back once at Aiden. He raised his chin to me.

"I won't give up, Tess," he called, his voice thick. "I'll make this up to you."

I blinked heavily, unwilling to listen, then yanked open the door to Joel's car.

"Looks like I missed a great party," Joel said as we drove toward my house. "I mean, ex-boyfriends on the lawn and cheerleaders running out into the streets. Sounds like a hoot."

"It was definitely unforgettable."

"Things involving you usually are."

My face warmed, and I looked sideways at him as he drove through the darkened streets. He was smiling, staring out the windshield. There were light splatters of rain on the glass as it started to drizzle, and Joel clicked on the wipers and turned up the heat. We didn't listen to the radio.

"I didn't know you were coming to the party," I said after a while of car silence. "Kira didn't mention it."

He looked sideways at me. "Uh...why would she?"

I scrunched my face, not sure what he meant. I opened my mouth to answer just as my phone vibrated in my pocket. I didn't know who it was, and there was no way I was going to look now. I turned to gaze out the window at the passing streetlights.

"So what did he want?" Joel asked, flicking on the turn signal and merging onto the highway.

"Aiden? To talk to me," I murmured. "To explain himself." My stomach turned as I thought about the pain on his face. The embarrassment.

"Did he explain himself?"

I didn't want to answer because I didn't want to believe it myself. And even though Aiden was the only person I'd ever slept with…he couldn't say the same. I might get sick.

I rolled down the window and let the wet air hit my face, probably wrecking my makeup and hair, but at this point, it didn't matter. Tonight changed everything.

"Our friendship is a problem for Kira," Joel said suddenly, his voice low. I opened my eyes in the air. Slowly I brought my head back in the car and rolled up the window.

"I know," I answered, looking down into my lap.

"But…" He paused and exhaled. "I don't want to stop being your friend, Tess." He glanced over at me. "I have a lot of fun with you." He smiled. "Even when your hair is sticking up in all directions and you have makeup smeared under your eyes."

I laughed, reaching up to smooth back the hair poking out on the sides. Then I swiped my fingers under my lids and sniffled. "Better?"

"Much."

I cleared my throat as Joel turned onto my street and pulled up to the curb in front of my house. When he stopped, he cut the engine. The streetlight above us illuminated the car so that I could see pretty clearly. I could see his hazel eyes.

"It was an unsolvable problem," he said as he exhaled, like he'd been waiting to tell me that.

I furrowed my brow, looking over at him. "I…" I wanted to tell him that Kira was out of control, that she was acting possessive and mean. "Joel, I'm not sure I'm the one to give you advice," I said instead.

He laughed. "That's probably true."

We sat together in his car, parked in the street and listening as the rain tapped on the windshield. I let the night wash over me. The copy-Kitten exposing the couples. How they stayed together. How Aiden had come for me.

"Aiden slept with someone else." I paused. "Would you forgive him?" I asked Joel, my head resting against the back of the seat as I watched the water pool and run down the driver's-side window.

Joel crossed his arms over his chest. "No."

I blinked quickly. I wished the rain would stop. It was completely depressing.

"I don't know what to do," I whispered.

"Not Chris Townsend," Joel answered, staring straight ahead.

"Nope. I pretty much burned that popularity bridge tonight, I think."

Joel laughed to himself. "It's kind of funny, me and you being all sad together. I'm pretty sure we're the nicest people I know."

I tsked and sat up, smiling at him. "You're not all that nice, Joel. You make fun of me nonstop."

He shrugged. "That's because you can take it. Kira hated my jokes. In fact, she didn't even think I was funny."

But I didn't believe that. His comedic timing was pure perfection; even Kira had to see that. But at the mention of her name, Joel seemed down again. I hated to see him like this.

"You and Kira are fine," I said to him, nodding. "You'll see."

Joel turned to me, his eyes nearly amber in the streetlight shine. "What do you mean?" he asked. "Tessa, I'm not sure you—"

My phone vibrated again, making me jump. I sighed, unable to fight it much longer, and pulled it out to look at the number. "It's Aiden," I murmured.

"Want me to tell him to piss off?" Joel asked with a smile, holding out his hand.

I laughed. "No, better not. You're way too classy for that."

"Right," Joel agreed. "Totally high class."

I slid the phone back and grasped the door handle. "Thank you for the ride," I said. "You saved me from humiliation."

"I did?" he said, snapping his fingers. "Darn."

I slapped his shoulder but then smiled. "I have to go in, okay?" The Smitten Kittens were probably wondering what had happened to me. I'd have to call them ASAP.

Joel smiled. "Okay. It's always nice talking with you, Tessa. You're a good friend." He reached out to swipe a damp strand of hair behind my ear, and I tensed as a shiver ran down my back.

My breath caught as his hand paused on my ear just a second longer than necessary. "Uh..." I stammered, blinking quickly. "Thanks." I pushed out into the rain, shutting the door quickly behind me.

My pulse was racing. I wasn't sure what had just happened, but when he touched me like that, I...I...

I dashed up my driveway and paused under the porch awning before looking over my shoulder to the road. Joel waved once to me before turning on his car and pulling back into the street. And while I watched him go, there was one thing I was sure of.

Just then, that feeling I had—it was a lot more than just friendship.

(CODE PINK) SOS
INTER-KITTEN COMMUNICATION

Dear Smitten Kittens,

Next weekend is the homecoming dance. We have a very sensitive sting operation in place to catch this knockoff Kitten, and please be mindful of your assigned position. This is one clever spy we're trying to catch. (And for the record, I think it's Mary Rudick. Just saying.)

Those of us not meeting at Tessa's house before the dance should have the equipment in place at the gym prior to her arrival. Also, make sure to have both the police and emergency personnel on speed dial. And Izzie, remember it's 9-1-1. Not 9-11. There is no 11 on the phone.

Good luck, Smitten Kittens. After this weekend, the real SOS will be back in business.

Keep smiling,

Leona ☺

CHAPTER NINETEEN

FOR THE ENTIRE WEEK, I KEPT MY DISTANCE FROM Joel, not just because it felt a little awkward now, but also because Kira shot me dagger stares every time his name was mentioned. Let's just say she wasn't all that appreciative of the ride home he gave me after the party—even when I'd explained myself three times.

And though at this point I had less than stellar feelings toward Mary, what she'd said about the drama—that the shift in captainship would strain mine and Kira's relationship—rang true. But having to pretend-cheat with Kira's boyfriend wasn't going to make it any better.

In reality, I was doing this for her, for all of us. It was my responsibility to catch the copy-Kitten and save our high school. That was what the Smitten Kitten skirt stood for. And if I had to fake it to make it, so be it.

The day of the dance, the Smitten Kittens were huddled in my bedroom while I got dressed. Even though we'd all gotten our hair and makeup done together, I was the only one in a gown. They were dressed in black for the mission, but it was still kind of cute with the dangling earrings and updos. When I came in from the bathroom, Izzie clapped.

"Tess, you look beautiful!"

I smiled. The dress I had was awfully pretty. My mother had surprised me with it the weekend before. Unfortunately my parents were in Seattle this weekend, but I promised to take lots of pictures. I didn't mention that some of the pictures would be of the spying variety.

My dress was a pale yellow with soft, shimmery fabric billowing out below my waist. Due to a conflict in the schedule, the homecoming game was moved to tomorrow, and luckily, between planning out this mission and navigating best-friend jealousy, I'd put together some fabulous cheers.

Leona looked over the top of the magazine she was reading as she lounged on my bed. "Looks better on you than it did while it was hanging up."

"Thanks," I said, blowing out a deep breath. In my depression, I'd ramped up my yoga routine, easily losing the five pounds to make this dress now look perfect. I missed my talks with Joel. And I wouldn't even begin to think about Aiden.

None of the other Smitten Kittens had a date to the dance. Marco had been seeing someone else, Sam had dumped Izzie, and Kira's boyfriend, well—we weren't allowed to talk about him in that context.

"Hey," Leona said, tossing the magazine on my bed as she sat up. "I need to talk to you about something."

Kira snickered and I could hear Izzie gulp. Never a good sign.

"Okay…" I was a little worried. Seemed like every time someone wanted to talk to me, it was terrible news. Why didn't people ever want to talk to me about good things? Like bunnies or cotton candy?

Leona looked into her lap, seeming uncomfortable, then

straightened up to meet my eyes. "I'll just say it." She exhaled, shaking her head. "Chris Townsend asked me to homecoming."

I gasped, completely surprised.

"Seems her little outfit worked," Kira said, playing with her hair in the mirror. "Guess you should have dressed up more, huh, Tess?"

That stung. I turned back to Leona. "Really? Wait, did you say yes?" I wasn't exactly offended or jealous that he'd asked her. Just…surprised.

"I did," Leona said, scrunching her nose. "Is that okay with you?"

I shrugged. "Yeah, I guess. I mean, I think he's a nice guy and all. I just…I didn't know you were into him."

Leona smiled a little to herself. "I didn't either. But after the fight and after you left, we started playing pool and…we just clicked. Did you know that he's planning on majoring in business next year?"

"No," I said. When I thought about it, there wasn't much I did know about Chris Townsend other than the fact that he was a good football player.

"He has a total five-year plan," Leona said, sounding way more interested than I could have thought possible.

"Well, I think it's spectacular," I said. "He's a total catch. I'm really happy for you, Leona." I smiled at her, completely proud that my Kitten had just found her Tom Cat. Leona grinned back and thanked me.

"Gets you off the hook," Kira said, applying some lip gloss. "Not that you liked him anyway." She looked over her shoulder at me, narrowing her eyes.

I felt like the curls in my hair were going to wilt next to the negativity that Kira was sending my way. I understood that she didn't want Joel involved with this operation, but truly, if she wanted to catch this copy-Kitten and move on with him, she needed to adjust her attitude. I sighed, turning away from her.

"Here's the plan," Izzie said as she sat crisscross applesauce in the pink beanbag in the corner of my room. She unfolded the itinerary that Leona had printed up for her. "In"—she checked her watch—"twenty minutes, Tessa will call Joel and tell him she has to speak to him urgently." She flicked an uncomfortable glance at Kira, but Kira wasn't listening. She was sitting on my desktop, painting her nails and blowing on them. Izzie cleared her throat and continued.

"Tessa will ask him to meet her under the bleachers in the gymnasium." Izzie paused to sigh. She looked at me wistfully. "That was the first place Sam kissed me."

"Stay on task," Leona said, rolling her eyes.

"Sorry. Okay, so Tessa will meet him under the bleachers. Before she gets there, we'll set our positions in the rafters and in the hallway, the back door and the school entrance. No way this copy-Kitten is getting in undetected."

"We're going to nail her," I said to Izzie, trying to sound brave.

Kira scoffed. "It's 'screw,' remember, Tess?"

I opened my mouth to correct her but then decided not to. I motioned with my hand for Izzie to continue.

"Well," she said. "Once the copy-Kitten intersects your call with Joel, they'll probably figure out a way to bug you or him. I mean, that's what we'd do, right?" She glanced around and we all nodded.

"So once you two are there...you're really going to have to

play it up." She winced a little. "You know this might end your friendship with him, right? I mean, you're sort of going to be throwing yourself at him."

I thought I heard a sound from behind me, but I didn't turn to Kira. I just nodded. I'd considered that, and even though I absolutely didn't like the idea of ending my friendship with Joel (especially by looking improper), I knew it was for the best.

I glanced over to Leona, who pressed her lips in a smile and nodded at me. "You'll be great, Tess," she said softly, possibly reading the sadness in my face.

"Thanks," I whispered.

"Wonderful. Now let's go over it one more time," Kira said, hopping down from the desk to grab her backpack from the floor and unzipping it. She'd finally agreed to help with this case, even though she clearly didn't want to. "I have the zoom lens, the binoculars, and the infrared camera. Leona has the rope packed in her car. My course is in the rafters."

"It'll be perfect," I said. Above the gym there was a walkway that the janitors had erected to get to the lights and ceiling during some recent renovations. It would be the prime spot to spy from. And since it was her boyfriend down there, Kira probably knew that.

"It's almost time," Izzie said, checking her watch. She and Leona exchanged a worried glance.

I took a steadying breath, glancing toward my phone where it sat on my side table. It was convenient that this year the dance would be held in the cafeteria. Not nearly as glamorous as a restaurant or even the gym, but it suited our situation well.

"Have you figured out what you're going to say yet?" Kira asked, trying to look disinterested.

"Sort of. I'm thinking of telling him something happened with Aiden and me? I don't know. Do you think that'll work?"

"Just be hot," Leona said, not looking up. "All guys care about is hot."

"Excuse me," Kira scoffed. "That's my boyfriend you're talking about."

"Right," Leona responded. "Then play dumb, Tessa. That seems to work."

I was about to scold her when the doorbell rang, startling me. I looked toward the door, my dress shifting with an adorable whooshing sound.

"Were you expecting someone?" Kira asked, maybe a little suspicious.

"No." And I really wasn't. With my eyebrows pulled together, I walked through my house and crossed the kitchen to the front door. I swung it open and gasped.

"Hi."

It was Aiden. He was standing there, unshaven, disheveled. Wait, was he wearing pajamas? I shook my head, as if to ask him what he was doing here.

"I know you don't want to talk to me right now," he said, his voice scratchy. "I know...you probably hate me. But I just wanted to see you before you went to the dance. You look beautiful."

I felt my cheeks blush, but I quickly pushed any affection I had away. I was about to start a mission. I couldn't let Aiden distract me.

"I can't talk to you right now," I said, folding my arms across my chest.

"Will you ever?" he asked back quickly. "Will you ever talk to me again?" He swallowed hard, his Adam's apple bobbing. "I'm going crazy, Tess."

I stared at him then, looked at him for a long moment before responding. I closed my eyes. "No. I don't think I will."

I couldn't see him, but I heard him let out a soft cry. There was a stabbing pain in my chest and I opened my eyes to look down at the fabric of my dress, wishing I could just spin around to watch it flow around me, forgetting about Aiden and Mary.

When I finally got up enough courage to look at him, his head was hanging, his hand was over his mouth. I saw tears drip from his cheeks to the ground. It was too much—watching this was too much right now. I needed to get back inside and call Joel.

"I'm sorry, I have to go," I said quickly, swiping under my eyes to make sure my makeup was safe. "Thanks for coming by, Aiden. But tonight's homecoming and…" I had started to go back inside when he reached out to take my arm.

"Tessa…"

"Have a good night," I said, pulling my arm out of his hand and not looking at him. "Goodbye, Aiden." My voice cracked on his name, but I swished my way through my door.

"I still love you, Tessa," Aiden called after me before I shut the door.

By the time I got back to my bedroom, my makeup was a lost cause. Once my ex-boyfriend set foot on my property, I was a goner. But the minute I walked in my room, I grabbed the box of tissues off my desk and began blowing.

"Who was it?" Kira asked, sounding annoyed.

"Aiden," I answered, my voice thick with tears.

"I still can't believe he went all the way with Mary," Izzie squeaked, getting up to come over to the bed and sitting next to Leona. She patted it for me for sit down too. I nodded, unable to talk as I blew my nose into the tissue.

"Well, Mary is pretty," Kira said from across the room. I looked up at her, blurry eyed.

"But in a skanky way," Leona added, smiling for support. "Like some other cheerleaders we know." Kira narrowed her eyes but didn't respond.

After another minute of feeling sorry for myself, I felt Leona's hand on my shoulder. "I know you're sad, Tess," she said. "But it's after seven. You have to pull yourself together. Let's finish this assignment and then we'll all set out on a new mission. To get boyfriends."

"Um, hello," Kira called. "I still have one."

"Yeah, whatever." Leona climbed off the bed and stood in front of me as I sat on the edge of my bed, tissue still covering my nose. "Sharpen up," Leona said, bending down to get close to my face. "Mission starts now."

With the Smitten Kittens' help, I managed to look halfway decent and lose my blotchy crying skin. We tweaked the plan, and I decided to call Joel once I got to the gym, making it a little easier for the copy-Kitten to intercept. Chances were, they were already following me.

I walked into the gymnasium, my heels clicking on the wood floors and echoing in the air. It was creepy. I knew that the girls were already here, arriving twenty minutes before me, but I didn't dare look toward them. In case the copy-Kitten was here, I didn't want to give up our position.

I sorted through my purse and pulled out my pink phone, dialing Joel's preprogrammed house number. He answered on the first ring, and I smiled. I loved promptness.

"Hello?" He sounded confused.

"Hi, Joel. It's Tessa."

"Really?" He laughed. "I thought you were avoiding me." I shifted in my heels, surprised he had noticed.

"I wasn't avoiding you. I was…busy."

"Busy avoiding me."

I twitched my nose, wondering if I'd hurt his feelings by not talking to him. I really didn't like the idea of that. "I'm sorry," I said.

"Fine. You're forgiven. But you owe me a vanilla Frappuccino."

I smiled, wishing I could just do this tonight—talk with a friend. But that wasn't part of the deal, and after tonight, Joel might never speak to me again.

I walked over to the wall, my heels clicking. I bent down to sit against it—even in my pale yellow dress. Once on the floor, I exhaled.

"Aiden came to see me today," I confided, only half acting.

The phone made a rustling sound on Joel's end. "Again? What did he say? Are you all right?"

"I don't know," I murmured. "I don't know anything anymore." I almost started crying, but I sniffled and straightened my back, ignoring the slight twitch there.

"He's being a jerk off," Joel said, sounding authentic. "He needs to leave you alone now."

I appreciated the protective tone in his voice. I let it soothe me.

"Is there anything I can do?" he asked softly.

Here it was, my chance. But for a second, I wanted to tell him to meet me somewhere else altogether and maybe go for corn dogs. There was a noise from above me.

I closed my eyes. "Can you meet me?" I asked, trying to focus on the mission. "I'm at the gym."

"What are you doing there?"

"It's a long story." And it certainly was.

"Um...You need me now?"

"Yes. Right now." I couldn't believe I was doing this.

Joel was quiet. Then, "I'll be there in ten minutes."

ASSIGNMENT 5

The operative bit off the ends of her red nails as she watched from the supply closet. It was a perfect view to where Tessa was standing under the bleachers. She looked nice, dressed up so delicately. It almost was enough to forget the fact that she was a liar.

The operative watched through her night-vision lens as Tessa talked on her phone, walking over to the wall to slide down to the ground. For a minute, the operative felt a small pang of regret, seeing the sadness on Tessa's face. But she pushed it away. Tessa had brought this upon herself.

Under the bleachers, Tessa clicked off her phone and dropped it to the floor next to her feet, exhaling loudly. She looked nervous.

She should. The operative just needed to get through this, and then she had a revenge planned that would be so much worse than what happened at the party. So much more damaging.

Tessa pushed herself up off the floor. She swiped at her dress with both hands, making sure it was clean.

For a second, the operative froze as Tessa's gaze touched on the half-open storage closet across from her. But a sound from the hallway made Tessa turn.

Just then, the door pushed open just enough for Tessa to react to who was about to enter.

She smiled.

CHAPTER TWENTY

I STOOD UNDER THE BLEACHERS OF THE HALF-
lit gymnasium in my homecoming dress waiting for Joel, my heart
pounding from both spy anxiety and the knowledge that I was
being watched. It definitely bothered me to be on this end of the
lens, and it made me wonder about all the subjects I'd investigated
in the past.

Kira and the other Smitten Kittens were surely watching from
above me in the rafters, but I didn't dare look up. No. The copy-
Kitten was here. I could feel it.

The gym door cracked open, sending in a streak of light.
"Tessa?" It was Joel. At the sound of his voice, my heart skipped
a beat underneath the flowy material of my dress and I smiled.

"Over here," I whispered, trying to sound like this was a casual
encounter. Joel saw me and nodded, walking inside and then closing
the metal gym door quietly. When it clicked shut, he slipped his
hands into the pockets of his suit and strolled my way.

I could tell from the grin on his face that he liked my dress.
He even sighed when he paused in front of me. "Wow, Tessa." He
shook his head. "You look gorgeous."

I widened my eyes, wary of Kira, who was hearing all this
and almost certainly not liking it. "Thanks," I said, trying to
punch his shoulder playfully. It just came out as awkward. I was
a terrible flirt.

"You're welcome, *pal*?" He laughed.

He was clueless as to what was going on, and I couldn't tell him. Instead I tried to pretend like I hadn't lost my mind. "I needed to talk to someone," I said, glancing away from him toward the ground. "And you're really good at listening." Well, that part was true.

Joel shifted, his loafers scraping the floor. "Don't take this the wrong way, but…you're not thinking of taking him back, are you? That would be really stupid."

My eyes snapped up as I stared at his soft hazel eyes, weighing his comments. "Why shouldn't I take him back?" My heart began to beat faster under the bodice of my dress. Joel was gazing at me, and I was mesmerized by his compassion, by the way he cared about how I felt. About my future.

"Because there could be someone else out there for you. Someone better."

I blinked heavily, and Joel laughed, self-consciously rubbing at his chin as he stepped closer to me. My breath quickened. He smelled good—a clean mix of soap and aftershave. His hair was brushed to the side, totally dapper.

"You look like you need a hug," Joel whispered, holding out his hand. It was trembling slightly, and I drew in a long breath, trying to convince myself that what I was about to do was for the Smitten Kittens. For an assignment.

I reached out, sliding my palm into his, feeling his heat envelop me. Very gently, he tugged me closer until we were almost touching.

Then he exhaled and put his arms around me, resting his chin on my head. It was a sweet gesture, but intimate. I felt myself melt into him.

"Kira's so lucky," I murmured with my eyes closed.

Joel's body tensed. "What do you mean?" He pulled back and looked down at me, confused.

Dang, was I blowing the mission? I shouldn't have brought her up. "Um…"

"Tessa," Joel said, his eyes narrowed. "You know that Kira and I broke up, right?"

I stepped away. "What? When?" My hands fell to my sides and I looked around the room, completely flabbergasted.

"Remember that day of the fair?" he asked. "That night…I told her that I didn't think it was working out. Wait. You didn't know? I thought that was why you were avoiding me."

"Joel, are you serious?" I started shaking my head, trying to rethink this. Joel and Kira were still together. She said so herself.

"Yeah, Tess," Joel murmured, moving closer to me. "I would have told you, but…I don't know. You were having problems with Aiden, and I didn't want to bother you with this."

My eyes darted around the room. Kira had been so jealous tonight, so possessive of him. The last week had been absolute misery for me, and yet she hadn't even mentioned that they'd broken up. This was a big deal. How could she not mention it? It affected the mission. It meant—

I froze. My clutch purse was lying on the floor and I picked it up, rummaging through it, looking for my phone.

"Tessa," Joel said, sounding concerned. "What's wrong?"

"Hold on." I sped through the numbers in my recent calls, and when I found Mary's, I clicked it.

"Hello?" she answered, sniffling. I cringed at the sound of her voice.

"Question," I started. "Why did you go to the squad and tell them not to let me back on?"

"Tessa!" She sounded completely relieved to hear from me, but I had no time for her apologies.

"Just answer me."

She paused. "I...I didn't think I had a choice. It had nothing to do with Aiden, I promise. Oh, Tessa. I'm so sorry. You have to know—"

"Then why did you tell the girls not to let me on the squad?" My heart was racing and I closed my eyes, scared of her answer.

"Kira," she said finally. "She told me you were out of control. Said you were running everything in the ground, but no one would listen to her. Asked me to help her. I...I believed her. Aiden said you'd changed too."

"Don't," I said quickly. "Don't you dare talk about him to me." I exhaled and opened my eyes, seeing Joel staring at me wide-eyed. "I have to go, Mary," I said. "We'll discuss this another time." Although I had no intention of following up on that offer.

I hung up the phone and slid it into my purse, then met Joel's concerned gaze. The reality of the situation hit me. "You should go," I said to him.

"What? But I'm here for you, Tessa. I came to see you." His voice got quiet and I felt him reach out to touch my hand. He smiled, looking nervous.

"Thank you," I whispered. "You're...a good friend." Joel seemed to wince at the word and slowly dropped my hand with a soft laugh.

"Yeah," he said, looking down at me tenderly. "You too."

"You should go," I repeated, wanting to get him out of here before the copy-Kitten was exposed. He didn't need to be involved in this. He wouldn't understand. "Go," I said, pushing him toward the exit.

Joel looked back at me, concerned, but then he nodded and made his way to the door. "I'll save you a dance, tiny Crimson," he said with a smile. And then he left.

Normally Joel's adorable words would have sent excited tingles over my body, but instead the rage of the moment began to fill me. And the minute the door clicked, I spun around to face the empty gymnasium.

After all these years and all this time…I closed my eyes, trying to let the shaking in my fingers subside. But my adrenaline was too keyed up. I opened my eyes and clenched my fists.

"Where are you?" I screamed, looking up to the empty rafters and then toward the back door. There was a scurrying sound above me until finally Leona appeared and came jogging toward me.

"What the hell, Tessa?" she said, a thick strap over her shoulder holding her new equipment. "We haven't caught the—"

"It's her," I said, my face on fire. "It's a flipping Kitten."

"Excuse me?" Leona said. "You mean Mary, right?"

I shook my head. "No." Suddenly there was a bang from the supply closet and I turned to face it. My blood was boiling. I wasn't sure I'd ever felt so angry in my whole life, not even at Chloe or Mary.

I began to cross the room to where the supply closet was shut, my heels clicking on the wood floor. Leona jogged to keep up with me. I looked sideways at her. "Where's the rest of the squad?"

"Checking the perimeter for accomplices. Kira thought they might have one waiting outside."

I laughed. She was a clever Kitten after all. Leona and I stopped in front of the supply-closet door and turned to look at each other.

"What is going on, Tess?" she asked, hitching up her eyebrow. "I'm totally freaking."

I straightened my posture, preparing to face what was behind door number one. Then I leaned forward to open the door that would reveal our imposter.

It was dark at first, and the room was silent, other than the sound of our ragged breathing. Then from the closet, there was a low laugh.

She stepped out, camera in hand. Her dimples set deep with a smile. I shook my head, barely able to believe it. I think part of me had hoped I was wrong.

"Kira?" Leona choked out, standing next to me. "What the hell?" Leona reached over to hook her arm in mine, pulling me backward as Kira glared at me from the shadows of the doorway.

She ran her hands down her curves, smoothing out her suit before stepping out into the gym. The buzzing lights above illuminated her just enough to make her look sinister.

"Don't look so stunned, Tess," Kira called, before her black high-heeled boots made clacking noises on the wood floor. She slowly began to cross the empty room toward us, wrapping one sleek boot in front of the other, almost like a zigzag.

The pulled muscle in my back was screaming at me, but I didn't react to it. I was too shocked. I was too betrayed. "But… why?" I asked her, my throat suddenly dry. "You were my best friend." The thought nearly made me cry.

Kira scoffed and shook her head. "Exactly. *Were.*" Then, as if seriously irritated, she quickened her pace in my direction. Her blonde curls were pulled tight in a bun, her makeup flawless, her lips ruby red. She was completely done up for homecoming—minus the dress and smile.

Leona tried to pull me away, but not before Kira was in front of me.

Slap! My face turned with the force of her hand across my cheek. I stepped back, shocked and stinging like all heck. I reached up to touch my face, my eyes wide and watering.

Leona stepped forward and shoved Kira hard enough to make her stumble back. "Have you lost your mind?" she screamed at her, but I was still standing there. Furious.

My best friend had just hit me. She *hit* me! I shook my head, clearing it. "K, th-that was completely uncalled for," I stammered, still feeling the burn on my cheek. "What have you done?"

"What you couldn't," she shot back, walking forward and knocking into Leona's shoulder with the side of her body on the way.

"Don't even think—" Leona started, holding up her finger in warning.

"Get the rest of the squad," I said to her. "We need backup. Tell them it's a severe case of post-traumatic SOS disorder." It was the only explanation.

"Oh, shut up, Tessa," Kira said, stopping to stand boot to heel with me in center court and snaking her neck. "Ever think that my problem is you? Ever think that maybe *you* were the one causing my stress?" She narrowed her eyes.

"Me?" I touched the front of my homecoming dress, completely offended. "You've been lying for weeks, Kira. Maybe longer!"

"I'll be right back," Leona said quickly, and then turned back to look at Kira. "With a straitjacket, you crazy bitch."

"Language," I mumbled, never taking my eyes off of Kira. Her hands were balled up into fists at her sides.

"Whatever I've done, K, it shouldn't have come to this. I just wanted us to move on with our lives—minus SOS."

"And my boyfriend? Were you planning on moving on with him?" Her blue eyes were wide with rage. I hardly recognized her.

"What? No?" But my voice squeaked, making my denial sound more like an admission of guilt. It was true: I hadn't planned on stealing Kira's boyfriend. I mean, yes, I had feelings for him, but I'd never planned that!

"You're no better than any of the cheaters we've ever followed," she hissed, holding my stare. She exhaled, blinking quickly. "When you ended SOS, I supported you. I trusted you, but then I saw that you were doing it for Aiden, not for us. Not for the girls of the school. And after I met Joel, I thought I could handle it all." She laughed self-consciously. "But I couldn't. And then every day I had to listen to people tell me, 'Why isn't Tessa leading the squad?' How do you think that felt? Then I thought, well, maybe if I let her on the squad, everyone will see how much better I am." She leaned in toward me. "I even tried to set you up with Chris to keep you out of trouble, and instead what do you do? You try to steal my boyfriend. Stabbed in the back by my best friend."

"Me? Kira, you were sneaking around spying on *me*! You broke into my house, and that was long before me and Joel—"

"He's mine!" she shouted.

"You can't own someone, Kira! And besides, you're not even going out anymore. He told me."

With an audible growl, she tackled me, her petite body crashing into mine and knocking us back and onto the floor. We landed with a thud onto the hardwood, sending a vibration up my arm as my elbow made contact.

For a second, we both just lay there. Neither of us was really a fighter. It was way too violent. "Ow," Kira said, rubbing at her forehead, which had smacked the ground next to me. She collapsed on the floor with a sigh, both of us breathing heavy. I turned to look sideways at her.

"I was captain," she groaned, sounding exhausted. "SOS was mine to fix. I was making it better."

"No," I said, wincing as I sat up. I looked at my elbow to see it was skinned, little scratches of blood beginning to show. "You were making it about vengeance. It was supposed to help people, not hurt them. And it's not your fault you were failing. SOS was a team sport, K. No one Kitten could have pulled it off alone."

She dropped her arms to her sides, staring up at the beams of the ceiling. "I wanted to stop cheaters. I wanted to make them pay."

"You were wrong," I said. "It was never the intent of SOS to exact revenge." But sitting here now, bruised and bloodied on the gym floor, I realized my part in this mess. I thrust the captainship on her, then abandoned her to figure it out on her own. I swallowed hard. "I'm sorry I wasn't there for you, K. I was wrong."

I rested my chin on my bare shoulder as I looked back at her. Her eyes snapped to mine, studying me, maybe checking to see if I was sorry. She sat up with a few pained grunts.

"You know, we still have some things to decide," she murmured. "SOS can't stop now. And even if you get back on the squad, they'll never trust you like they used to."

I nodded. "I have some things to make up for," I admitted. "And now that people know about SOS, they'll never stop searching for us. Not unless we can prove we stand for good."

"Maybe my way is better," she said, glancing toward me.

"It's not." I watched her as she smiled a little, like she was going to challenge everything from here on out.

"I'm still the captain of the Smitten Kittens," she said.

I couldn't believe that after everything she'd done, all the lying, she was still adamant about being the captain. I felt anger course through me.

"Oh," I said. "You're hereby relieved of captain duty. And possibly off the squad. I'll let the Smitten Kittens vote on it."

"Go for it. Some of them will stand with me."

I considered this. "Not all of them." But she was right. The squad would be split, and that was no way to cheer. I'd need to figure out a way to bring us back together. Fake friends for the sake of school spirit. At least for a little while.

"Co-captains, then?" I asked, my elbow throbbing.

Kira sneered. "One more thing for us to share."

"After a mandatory suspension, of course. Let's say the rest of the football season. We'll see you during basketball." It was a harsh sentence, but really, she didn't have room to complain. She was lucky I wasn't calling the police.

The gym doors opened with a metal click, and Leona came rushing in followed by Izzie and the rest of the squad. They skidded to a stop when they saw Kira and me sitting on the floor of center court.

"You okay?" Leona called to me. I waved, letting her know I was. At least physically.

Kira smiled, but I knew that smile. It was completely fake—totally inauthentic. It made my heart sink because right then I knew. I knew that things between Kira and me would never be the same.

"Kira's going to be suspended for the season," I announced, still sitting down. "She's admitted fault, and we hope to just move on from here. Repair the squad."

There was a series of murmurs and quiet patters as the team crossed the gym in their spying outfits.

"But I'll be back soon," Kira said, like it wasn't a big deal. "Co-captain for basketball. You all know I love you and I won't abandon you." She looked sideways at me.

Ooh…that really peeved me, but I was trying to keep a brave face. Leona shot Kira a dirty look, then outstretched her hand to mine.

I took it, smiling and blinking back my tears. She was choosing me. She was on my side of the foul line. When I tried to stand up, I was lopsided. I looked down at my foot, noticing that one of my shoes was missing. I glanced around quickly, but it was nowhere in sight. I'd wondered if it had flown under the bleachers when I'd been tackled.

Kira tsked as she slowly climbed up, smoothing back her blonde hair with her hands and avoiding eye contact. "Whatever," she mumbled.

Izzie stood apart from all of us, looking between Kira and me. She chewed on her lip, switching from foot to foot.

"Izzie—" I started, but she shook her head.

"I'm sorry, Tess," she whispered, dropping her eyes and crossing the court to stand behind Kira.

My mouth opened, and I was wounded, betrayed. But I didn't say anything. She'd made her choice.

"She can't help you get Sam back," Leona said to her, obviously as bothered by Izzie's lack of loyalty as I was.

"We'll see," Kira answered for her. Looking back over her shoulder to Izzie. "Sam isn't out of the picture yet." She smiled at her, then glanced at me. "Unless Tessa wants him, of course."

"Oh, shove it!" Leona said, and I had to reach out to hold her back. I couldn't believe that this was what we'd dissolved into. It was tragic. Complete *Death of a Salesman* tragic.

"The fake SOS is over now," I said to all of them, rolling back my shoulders. "Look, we all make mistakes, but we can't hold animosity toward each other. School spirit is on the line. We have to stick this landing and get through this."

"I'm glad you're back," Leona replied, her voice crisp. Then she smiled. "Without a leader, we were just Kittens. You brought the Smitten."

"You had a leader," Kira snapped, darting a glance her way.

Leona shook her head. "I have one now." Leona turned her back to Kira and looked at the rest of the girls. "Tessa's right. We need to let this go. We are not rogue Kittens. None of us should do things against the squad. No matter how jealous we might get." She smiled. "Now. Let's get back to that homecoming dance."

"Yes, let's," Kira murmured.

Leona spun around and tilted her head, studying Kira. "I don't know about you, but I have to go home to change. You're not going to wear that, are you?" Leona asked with a smirk, motioning to Kira's black outfit that was now covered in dust.

"No," Kira hissed. "My dress is in my locker."

"Classy."

I watched Kira's jaw clench, but then she began to brush the dirt from the gymnasium floor off of her clothes. Izzie chewed on her lip, looking between Kira and me, and then she shrugged.

"So we're still a squad?" she asked, her voice meek.

"Yes." I nodded, although I wasn't sure if that was true anymore. But for now, I'd have to pretend it was.

"Great." Izzie exhaled, rubbing her stomach. "I'm starving."

I pressed my lips together, nodding for the squad to go ahead, waiting until Kira and I were alone again. We turned to look at each other.

"One other thing," Kira said, focusing her big blue eyes on me. "I..." She paused, looking uncomfortable with what she was about to say. "I love him."

I swallowed hard and nodded.

"I love him, Tessa. So..." She looked away and then back at me. "So leave him alone, okay?"

My face stung. Not just because my ex-best friend had practically accused me of trying to steal her boyfriend, but also because...she was right to worry. And I knew that.

"I'll leave him alone." I nodded, wishing that things could go back to the way they were. But Kira and I were like SOS. We'd have to rebuild—even if we could never get to where we'd been before.

SOS
IMPORTANT ANNOUNCEMENT

Dear Clients,

This is an important announcement regarding SOS and its future dealings. During the last few months, an imposter infiltrated SOS. The situation has been handled, and the proper investigators are back on duty.

In the meantime, the real SOS has reinstated its former leader and is getting back to basics. We are a nonprofit organization and exist only on donations from our benefactors. In addition, there will be no more revenge, although matchmaking is still a possibility.

We are also returning to our top-secret status, and you can be assured that all the information collected will remain confidential. Although we are still trying to get the previously loaded videos off of YouTube.

SOS is looking forward to salvaging our reputations and rebuilding your trust.

If you suspect your boyfriend in a cheat, please send a cheater request to 555-0101.

Keep smiling,
SOS ☺
SOS
Text: 555-0101 * Exposing Cheaters for Over Three Years

CHAPTER TWENTY-ONE

WHEN I HOBBLED INTO THE CAFETERIA (STILL minus a shoe), my emotions were completely tied in lopsided bows. I stood, looking over the student body, unsure of where to begin.

Maybe it was the paper flowers or homecoming ribbons on the walls or the alternating red and blue lighting, but this place was romantic. And I didn't belong here. Not without Aiden.

I reached down to slip off my other shoe before making my way back out of the dance and down the deserted hallway. The sound of music slowly faded behind me, and I wondered where I should go. What I should do.

But going home didn't sound glorious, and the Smitten Kittens were all inside, enjoying their nights. And I wouldn't bring them down. Not when we'd finally solved the copy-Kitten crisis. Only they didn't know the real devastation. I'd have to fake it until we make it. No matter how much it hurt.

I paused and looked through the glass window of the exit door. I could see the filled parking lot, the streamers hanging on the cars for the parade at the end of the dance. It was so peppy that I had to smile.

I pushed hard on the heavy metal door and had made my way across the cement when I spotted the football field behind the parking lot. I laughed at myself. How obvious—where else would a cheerleader go to think?

When I got there, I sat down on the cool metal bleacher, looking out at the pieces of confetti littering the football field to prep it for the celebration. There was a chill in the air, so I wrapped my arms around my torso and glanced up at the scoreboard. Wildcats vs. Ducks. Even though I hadn't been a cheerleader in months, my school spirit had never faded.

I closed my eyes as a gust of wind blew through my hair, sending it back from my face. Behind my lids, I could feel tears, hot, salty.

Aiden was gone. He didn't belong to me anymore, and really, maybe he never had. Maybe we just weren't right, no matter how much we felt like we were. And even though I missed him, I didn't miss the confusion.

And Kira. I shook my head, not wanting to think about what she'd done, the ways she'd betrayed me. After all of our time together, she'd written me off. She wanted to hurt me.

I put my hands over my face, trying to block out the questions. The lies. Suddenly I felt something warm wrap around me and I spun around to see Joel standing there.

"Sorry," he said, smiling slightly. "You just look cold."

"I am." Inside and out. But it was certainly nice to see him.

He adjusted his coat around my shoulders before stepping over the bleacher and sitting down next to me. His thigh pressed against mine, and I wondered if he realized how close he was.

I slipped my arms into the sleeves of the jacket and used my fingertips to hold it closed. Even with company, my heart was still aching. Joel shifted next to me and I looked over at him.

The wind blew his brown hair around, and when he smiled,

warm and imperfect, I felt myself smile back. "Hi," he whispered, like we'd just started talking.

"Hi."

"You left the dance," he said, running his glance down the length of my dress to my bare feet. "Did you lose your shoe, Cinderella?"

I didn't want to tell him that his girlfriend had freaked out and physically assaulted me. Instead, "I lost it in the gym."

Joel nodded. "That's sort of funny," he said. I raised my eyebrow, not quite sure what could be funny about me walking around barefoot, holding my remaining shoe.

Joel reached over, and my heart sped up as he slipped his hand into the pocket of his coat (which just so happened to be against *my* body).

"I went back to the gym to look for you and…wait," he said, close enough that his breath was warm against my face. "It's not midnight, is it?"

"No," I murmured, not sure how to move anymore. Because I was fairly certain I should pull back in some way. Instead I sat there, nearly lip to lip with Kira's ex-boyfriend.

"Good," he whispered. "I wouldn't want you turning into a pumpkin or anything."

Okay, if Joel was drinking, I would probably have been able to smell it on his breath at this distance. But he seemed completely lucid. Completely—

Just then he pulled his hand out of his jacket pocket (which, again, had been against *my* body the entire time) and held up a shoe. My shoe.

"I found your glass slipper," he said with a huge smile on his face.

I looked between Joel and my yellow size six and a half and felt my entire body tingle. He shouldn't be here with me. He shouldn't be rescuing my shoe.

"Thank you."

"Does this mean I'm Prince Charming?" he asked, licking his lips as he glanced at mine. "I can slay a dragon if you need me to."

I stared into his soft hazel eyes, feeling both lost and safe. "No dragons in *Cinderella*," I murmured, my breath quickening.

"Yeah." He smiled. "I never believed in that fairy-tale bullshit anyway." Joel leaned over like he was about to kiss me. Then he moved his head and gently pressed his lips to my cheek, touching me so softly that for a minute, I wasn't sure if it was real.

I shut my eyes, aware that being this close to my ex-best friend's ex-boyfriend in the bleachers of the football field was completely unethical, both socially and athletically. But the way Joel touched me was so right. It was exactly what I needed, maybe all along.

With a whisper of a kiss, he pulled back only to rest his forehead against mine, his warm breath tickling my face. "I'm such a chicken," he said with a quick laugh.

There was another breeze and I felt the rush of air on my toes. Straightening up, I glanced at my high heel, still in Joel's hand. I smiled. "Would you mind?" I asked, crossing my legs to hold my bare foot in his direction.

He stared at my toes for a long moment, then scrunched his nose and looked over at me. "Actually, I do." He held out my shoe to me. "I have a weird thing with feet. They sort of gross me out."

I gasped, not because it was a horrible thing, but because it was a *different* thing.

"Not that your feet are gross," Joel said quickly, looking like he was worried. "I'm not saying that. They are very cute feet." He cringed a little. "It's just…I don't like anyone's feet. I…I'm just going to shut up now." He laughed and handed me my shoe.

Slipping it on quickly and then adding the other, I placed both feet back onto the floor of the bleachers and looked up as Joel examined them. "See, now they look cute."

"Oh, thanks."

Joel narrowed his eyes, glancing over me adorably. "You like me, don't you?"

I met his eyes without lifting my head. "Maybe."

He grinned. "'Maybe' means you're incredibly in love with me."

"Let's not get ahead of ourselves," I said. If there was one word I wouldn't throw around again, that was it. In fact, there was a good chance I'd never love anyone again.

"'Ahead of ourselves' means you want to jump my bones right here in the Washington High bleachers." He held up his hands. "But I'm sorry, Tess. I'm not that kind of boy."

"Stop." I laughed. Okay, maybe "never love again" was a bit overdramatic. "You know, you're sort of funny?" I asked, taking a strand of my hair and twisting it like I was bored. "You should really think about becoming a stand-up comedian or something."

Joel made a face and then smiled. "I have a better idea," he said, standing up and extending his hand to me.

I was scared to take it. What if my back spasmed again? What if—

"Take my hand," he whispered, his face becoming serious. "Be with me."

My stomach fluttered with anxious butterflies. He was right. I did like him. Without thinking anymore, I slid my cool palm into his, immediately comforted by his warmth. Joel pulled me to my feet and stood me up close to him. Carefully he put his hands on either side of my waist as I put my hands behind his neck.

"May I have this dance?" he asked.

I looked around the empty bleachers and the field beyond. "Here?" There weren't even any paper flowers!

"Right here."

I stared at him, seeing both his affection for me and his insecurity that I might walk away at any moment. And to be honest, I knew I should.

"Right now," he added, pulling me just a little closer.

Being against him and enjoying it were wrong. But I couldn't stop myself even if I tried. There were things I'd done in my past that I wasn't proud of. All the time with SOS, Christian, and some of my poor relationship choices with Aiden. And even as I stood, slow dancing in the bleachers, feeling completely…well, smitten, I had a feeling that out of any of my mistakes, this could wind up being my worst one.

Totally and completely falling for my ex-best friend's ex-boyfriend.

SOS
INTER-KITTEN COMMUNICATION

Dear Smitten Kittens,

The roster is posted, naming the new candidates for the squad. You'll see the list reprinted below. The tryouts will be held this Saturday at 9:00 a.m. in the gymnasium.

Candidates:

Chloe Ferril

Maureen Sarver

Sara Fricola

Anne Lancing

All Smitten Kittens (even the suspended ones) are expected to attend and vote. Don't be late.

Keep smiling,

Leona ☺

FROM: Aiden Wilder baller8@wsu.edu
TO: Tessa Crimson smittenkitten@yahoo.com
SENT: Sunday, September 30, 1:01 a.m.
SUBJECT: STILL WAITING

When you're ready to talk, I'll be here. I won't give up, Tess.
I love you.
Aiden

ACKNOWLEDGMENTS:

Disclaimer: The same ex-boyfriends that were not harmed in the writing of book 1 were also not harmed in the writing of *So Many Boys*. However, some of the emotions in the situations may or may not reflect feelings the author could have possibly experienced at some point in her life.

First, I have to thank Melissa Sarver for her continued patience and dedication to this series. And always knowing how to talk me down when I freak myself out.

My editor Anne Heltzel, who worked tirelessly on this project. You make my chest ache! And of course all of the wonderful folks at Razorbill, thank you for supporting me and my neurotic tendencies. And for promising me gold stars!

I'm incredibly lucky to be surrounded by supportive, brilliant friends. First, Heather Hansen, who is never afraid to tell me the truth and who is always there to sing my praises. You make me a better person. Amanda Morgan, a smiling face that always cheers me up and reminds me of who I am. Trish Doller, just about the best person in the world to write with, is completely inspiring. Daisy Whitney, your brilliance makes me feel like an awful writer, but it also makes me work harder. And some great friends: Lisa Schroeder, Laini Taylor, and all the amazing authors that have made Portland home.

Thanks to the Tenners, an amazing group of debut authors who continue to support me and listen to the highs and lows of the biz. The very cool bloggers that have gotten me excited about my own books with their never-ending charm. The musers who listen to my complaints. And the great businesspeople who have always offered me advice throughout the process: Alice Pope, Jen Rofe, Jordanna Fraiberg LeVine, and Laura Schechter.

Thank you all for investing your time in me. I hope I make you proud.

Finally, my love belongs with my family. My wonderful, sometimes funny husband, Jesse. (Just kidding, honey. *Always* funny.) And my equally entertaining children, Joseph and Sophia, who never let me take myself too seriously. My mother, Connie, and my sisters, brothers, cousins, and all you other folks who share DNA with me . . . THANK YOU.

And as always, to my grandmother: You are always with me, and I still miss you every day. Thank you for giving me permission to take chances.